P'TITES LURES GUERNÉSIAISES

Cover photograph courtesy of Brian Green

P'tites Lures Guernésiaises

*A Collection of Short Stories
in Guernsey-French
and English*

Edited
by
Hazel Tomlinson

ELSP

Published in 2006
Reprinted in 2007 by
ELSP
16A St John's Road
St Helier
Jersey   JE2 3LD

All enquiries and correspondence regarding this book
please direct to the editor
Hazel Tomlinson
Windy Ridge
Albecq
Castel
Guernsey   GY5 7HN

Origination by Seaflower Books

Printed by Cromwell Press
Trowbridge, Wiltshire

ISBN 1 903341 47 7

CONTENTS

FOREWORD

by Mr A C K Day
Patron of L'Assembllaïe D'Guernésiais

As a simple *fichu Angllais* it is a great privilege to be formally associated with L'Assembllaïe D'Guernésiais; equally to be asked to pen a few words in foreword to this splendid work, published to celebrate the 50th anniversary of L'Assembllaïe. Mrs Tomlinson is to be warmly congratulated on her efforts in assembling all the contributions and displaying her skills as general editor, and everyone who played a part in creating this worthy finished product. It cleverly assembles a collection of pièces which cover a wide range of subject matter, and, interestingly in my view, displays the variety of ways in which what is essentially a spoken language may still be written today. So, with grateful acknowledgements to that distinguished teacher Dr Tomlinson, and in great trepidation, I add a few words of my own.

Not'île peut mourtair que sa vieille langue est parlaie, et écrite – et à moins aen p'tit peu plloine de vie – et que ichin en Guernési nos rachines saont normandes accore. J'espère que chute collection dès pieces peut augmentair aen interêt dans not'culture et not'histouaire. Toutes les communautaies aont besougn d'enne identitaie. Comme a dit Ralph Vaughan Williams, "Without local loyalties, there is nothing to build on."

Je félicite les sians qu'aont bian travailli pour maette ensemble chutt'oeuvre, que j'espère s'en va aver aen bouan success. Je la recommende énn amas.

ACKNOWLEDGEMENTS

I am indebted to the following authors or their families who willingly gave me permission to include their work in this book, some of which were written for the Guernsey-French Eisteddfod during the last few years.

In alphabetical order: Mrs P Collenette, Mrs M De Garis, Mrs N Duquemin, the family of Mr P J Girard, Mrs E Green, the family of Mr T A Grut, the family of Mr A Heaume, the family of Mrs D O Heaume, the family of Mr J Hervé (Joe du Moullin), Mr B Hockey, Mrs R Jehan, Mr R H Langlois, the family of Mr H le Cheminant (Helier de Rocquoine), La Société Guernésiaise (for the pieces by Miss M Ozanne,), the family of Mr E M Renouf, the family of Mr T H Renouf, (Tom du Camp du Roi), the family of Mr G O Robilliard, Mr T Snell, Mrs M Squires-Beausire, Dr H Tomlinson and Mrs M Torode.

When invited by the Assembllaïe D'Guernésiais to be the patron of the society, Mr A C K Day accepted with enthusiasm and is a staunch supporter. I thank him for his remarks in the foreword.

I was delighted when my nephew, Paul Torode, agreed to produce some black and white sketches to illustrate several of the stories. As a former graphic artist and having been brought up in Torteval, he was able to capture some of the essence of Guernsey humour, and I am most grateful to him.

I am also very grateful to Mr Lloyd Le Tocq for having helped me to find pieces by authors who are perhaps less well-known.

My thanks go to the National Trust of Guernsey for permission to use the Folklore Museum at Sausmarez Park as a backdrop for the cover photograph by Brian Green of Cynthia Lenormand, Olive Sarre and myself in Guernsey costume.

I am also deeply indebted to my husband Harry who has encouraged me and given me practical help when I needed it. He has an extensive knowledge of Guernsey-French, Anglo-Norman and linguistics and is very keen to preserve what is left of our language.

I hope that I have not omitted anyone to whom I owe a debt of gratitude. If this is the case, I hope that they will accept my sincere thanks.

Finally, I would like to thank the Committee of L'Assembllaïe D'Guernésiais for the help and encouragement I have received in the compilation of this book to mark the 50th anniversary of its foundation.

PREFACE

About three years ago, I had the idea of collecting as many short pieces written in Guernsey-French by different authors as I could find. The original idea was to create an archive, but this soon changed to a collection of stories which could be published so that anyone interested in our ancient language would have easy access to the works of local authors.

Guernsey-French has its origins in Latin and is part of the development of Norman-French. The geographic isolation of Guernsey has led to certain peculiarities in its evolution. Whilst sufficiently similar to the languages of Normandy and Jersey to allow mutual comprehension, it is a language unique to the island. Even though it is essentially a spoken language, if it is not recorded in a written form, it will disappear eventually. However there is some interest in Guernsey-French outside the island and I hope that this collection will generate even more out there and within Guernsey too.

I was fortunate to find short stories by a number of authors in the *Bulletin de l'Assembllaïe d'Guernésiais* produced by that society since it was founded in 1956. It had two aims; a) to conserve as much of our native language as possible before it disappears completely and b) to try and perpetuate our customs and traditions which are in danger of being forgotten. I also traced other stories which are included in this collection with the help of Mr Lloyd Le Tocq.

Since the inception in 1956 of the Assembllaïe, we have indeed lost a number of our traditions and certainly our native language is under threat, although efforts are being made to preserve it for a while longer. Once it is no longer a spoken language, there will be only written records and tape recordings for students of minority languages to study, and I hope that this collection of short stories will help in their studies.

It must be remembered that many authors have used slightly different spellings from the others in this book. In the nineteenth century, George Métivier (from the Castel) and Denys Corbet (from the Forest) both wrote poetry in Guernsey-French based mainly on modified standard French. Métivier also produced a *Dictionnaire Franco-Normand* in 1870 which was the first of its kind to be produced. Before the *Dictiounnaire Angllais-Guernésiais* was compiled by the *Dictionary Committee of L'Assembllaïe d'Guernésiais* led by Mrs.Marie de Garis (first impression 1967, revised 1982), modern writers either used standard French spelling or a semi-phonetic version of their own devising. Some sounds in Guernsey-French do not exist in either French or English and it is sometimes impossible to reproduce them in the written word. Readers will notice that there may be several spellings of the same word by various authors, and this is because they came from different parts of the island and the pronunciation was different in that parish. This difference still exists today, eg. the accent and pronunciation of the Vale and Castel parishes, (in the north, Le Bas Pas) differ quite markedly from those in the western parishes – Torteval, St. Pierre du Bois, St. Saviour's and Forest, (Le Haut Pas).

I have tried to reproduce all the stories exactly as written by the authors, but in some cases there were obvious typing errors or, in the case of hand-written pieces, it was difficult to read the writing and I had to use my judgement. All the stories have been translated into English and I have tried to keep as closely as possible to the original texts.

H N Tomlinson
Albecq, Castel, Guernsey
2006

The Stories

In the following pages, the stories are presented as parallel text. The original Guernsey-French is given on the left-hand page, the English translation on the right. Where the story continues from one page to another this is indicated as follows: ☞

1

Au shaoux du Vouest
par Peggy Collenette

Mess Gaudiaon et sa faume la Sophie decidirent qui voulais allai au shaoux du Vouest.

Ils tais oblligi prumierement de prende enne bosse pour la ville, et en prend enn'aoute d'la ville allai a L'Eree, et ils tais tous fiar dauve laeu tour.

Mess Gaudiaon voulait vais les legeumes, parce qui l'tait raide interessi la dans. Les v'la allair dans la tente.

"Mais Sophie, quand nous vait toutes les tablle," et il'entrirent justement au but que les legeumes etais. Quand nous vait les belles paunais et les manifique carottes. Ches des carottes craeuse dans du sabllon, j'en sie saeure."

Y avait enn'affaire qui troubllait Mess Gaudiaon chaque pas qui faisais; y avait en haomme qu'etait a les siere, et ecoutait shu qui s'ente disais.

Quand i vinrent au but des tablles, Mess Gaudiaon dit a la Sophie, "J'sis bian caontent dauve shu qu'j'ai vaeux. V'la enne belle arlevaie."

L'haomme qui les sievait s'introduisit a Mess Gaudiaon.

"Men naom ches Mess Brehaut, et j'ai des bian millaeure legeumes que shena."

"Mais mourtai me vos legeumes, Mess Brehaut."

"Ah! Mais j'en ai pas mit au shaoux."

"Eh bian, si vous voulai pas maette au shaoux pour les juges a les vais, faut pas vous vantai ishin!"

1

At the West Show
by Peggy Collenette

Mr Gaudion and his wife Sophie decided that they wanted to go to the West Show.

First they were obliged to take a bus to Town, and to take another from Town to go to L'Eree, and they were very pleased with their tour.

Mr Gaudion wanted to see the vegetables because he was very interested in them. So they went into the tent.

"Oh Sophie, look at all these tables," and they went in just where all the vegetables were. "Look at the beautiful parsnips and the magnificent carrots. They are carrots grown in sand, I'm sure."

There was one thing which bothered Mr Gaudion each step that he took, there was a man who was following them and listening to what they said to each other.

When they came to the end of the tables, Mr Gaudion said to Sophie, "I'm very pleased with what I have seen. It's been a good afternoon."

The man who was following them introduced himself to Mr Gaudion.

"My name is Mr Brehaut, and I have much better vegetables than that."

"Well, show me your vegetables Mr Brehaut."

"Ah! but I haven't put any in the show."

"Well then, if you don't want to put any in the show for the judges to see, you mustn't boast about them here."

2

Célébraïr 25 onnaïes
par Peggy Collenette

Jimmin et Marie étais à célébraïr 25 aens de marriage, mais pour la Marie, ch'tai 25 aens de misère durant la niet. A dit à sa vaisaene, "Shu caoue j'en ait yaeux assai."

"Mais Marie, tchi-qu't'as daon?" dit la vaisaene.

"Mais ch'es Jimmin, sa raonfll'rie me garde évillie toutes les nietties, et j'en sie bian onniaïe. J'l'ait co-d'piaït, j'l'ai pinchi, et accore i raonflle. Jenne'sais pas daoute tchi faire, jenne peux pas daoute l'enduraïr."

"Ah!" dit la vaisaene, "Quand Jimmin parle d'allaïr s'coushier, va à la corde à linge tcheure enne épile à linge, et quand Jimmin s'ra bian endormi, met l'épile à linge à son naïz, et j'sis saeure que v'là qui f'ra la trique."

Marie dit à Jimmin, "Ve-iaon Jimmin, faut allaïr s'coushier. Il est temps."

Jimmin était tout fiar d'allaï s'coushier, et i n'fut pas bian laongtemps d'vant d'se maette à raonfflaïr.

La Marie n'le mantchi pas, al'avait l'épile à linge sous l'orillier, et a lie pinshi l'naïz autour l'épile et v'là la raonfll'rie qu'arrête.

La Marie et Jimmin dormisirent toute la niet et Jimmin s'éville au matin dauve l'épile à sen naïz.

Comme i dit, "Mais Marie, tchi qu't'as fait à mon naïz?"

"Ah!" dit la Marie, "j'ait iaeux la millaeure niet que j'avais iaeux pour 25 aens."

Celebrating 25 years
by Peggy Collenette

Jimmy and Marie were celebrating 25 years of marriage, but for Marie it was 25 years of misery during the night. She said to her neighbour, "This time, I have had enough."

"But Marie what's the matter?" said the neighbour.

"It's Jimmy, his snoring keeps me awake every night, and I am really fed up. I have kicked him, I've pinched him, and still he snores. I don't know what else to do, I can't stand it anymore."

"Ah!" said the neighbour, "when Jimmy talks about going to bed, go to the washing-line to fetch a clothes-peg, and when Jimmy is fast asleep, put the clothes-peg on his nose, and I'm sure that it will do the trick."

Marie said to Jimmy, "Come on Jimmy, let's go to bed. It's time."

Jimmy was very pleased to go to bed and it wasn't long before he began to snore.

Marie did not miss her chance, she had the clothes-peg under the pillow, and she pinched his nose with the peg and the snoring stopped.

Marie and Jimmy slept all night and Jimmy woke up in the morning with the peg on his nose.

He said, "But Marie, what have you done to my nose?"

"Ah!" said Marie, "I have had the best night's sleep that I've had for 25 years."

D'la gâche de Guernési
par *Peggy Collenette*

Avous oui l'histouaire de not gâche de Guernési?

La vieille Louise était embarrassaïe à faire sa pâte pour sa gâche, et v'là daon aen tappe à l'hus.

"Ah maon dou sécours, quaï tripot!" pensit la Louise." Et ma pâte est toute prête pour la maette à l'vaï, mais a s'en va refreger," et a trashi vite aen torshaeux pour couvri sa pâte. Le cat était corlaïr dans sa tchair, qui fait al'eputchit l'cat, et le pieshi dans la bole que la pâte était d'dans, et le cat s'coushit bian su la pâte, et a s'en fut repoande le tappe à l'hus.

Ah, ch'est ma vaisaene, la Marie.

"Entraï."

Ils d'visirent pour enne haeure, mais la Louise était pas chagrinaïe au tour sa pâte, pasqué a savait que le cat était à gardaïr la pâte caoude.

Quaend la Marie die "A la pershoine," la Louise r'gardit a sa pâte et dit, "Ches ishin la millaeure pâte que jait jomais fait."

Enne affaire, y avait aen p'tit d'plleau du cat su la pâte, mais la gâche était manifique.

About Guernsey Gâche *
by Peggy Collenette

Have you heard the story about our Guernsey Gâche?

Old Louise was busy making her dough for her gâche, and there was a knock at the door.

"Oh goodness gracious, what a to-do," thought Louise, "and my dough is all ready to put to rise, but it will get cold," and she looked for a tea-towel to cover her dough. The cat was curled up in its chair, so she picked up the cat and put it in the bowl in which the dough was, and the cat lay down comfortably on the dough, and she went to answer the knock on the door.

Ah, it's my neighbour, Marie.

"Come in."

They talked for an hour, but Louise was not worried about her dough, because she knew that the cat was keeping the dough warm.

When Marie said "Goodbye," Louise looked at her dough and said, "This is the best dough that I have ever made."

One thing, there was a little cat fur on the dough, but the gâche was marvellous.

---

* Guernsey gâche is a fruit loaf, eaten with or without butter. Gâche is the word for cake unless the type of cake is specified.

4

Ennn p'tite ôlure
par Marie De Garis

Enne arlevaïe la Judie décidi d'allaïr r'viraïr ciz la Rachael. Ils avaient étaï amis pour pus-s-qué chinquànte ans, dépis qui c'menchirent la p'tite école sus Les Buttes lé mesme jour. Y avait enne p'tite faene bllâze, mais ch'tait chose dé rian. La Rachael fut bian fière dé la veies et i s'assiévirent les daeux sus l'lliet d'fouaïlle à ouvraïr. La Judie avait prins sa caouche coum dé couteume et la Rachael était à faire aën corset d'oeuvre pour s'n haomme. Les aidjules naviguais autant coum leurs langues quand i s'enter caontais les drôines nouvelles dans la paraesse.

La Rachael sé l'vis à faire du thée. En versant enne coupaïe pour la Judie all'y dis, "O-tu, i faout qué j'te dit tchi qui s'arrivit l'aoute seraïe à la gniet au n'vaeu dé mon biau-frère. Il'tait sus son moto-byke lé laong d'la route du Vazaon et saïs-tu tchi qui vis? Aën barbou!"

"Oh mais noufait daonc," s'fit la Judie, "aën barboue? Quaï sort dé barboue? J'pensais pas daoute qu'avait rian ditaï tchéchis en Guernési. Dis-mé tout atour."

"La bête qui vit était daeux caoups aussi grànd qué lé pus grand tchen. Il avait des laongues oreilles pouôintu coum des caones. Et l'animal marchait daonc seulement sus ses pids d'derrière, et des iaers coum des sauciers."

"Cré-tu qu'il avait iaeux p'tête enne p'tite goute dé trop, ou fumaï tchique drogue et qu'i saongait?" dit la Judie.

"Nen-nin," répounit la Rachael. "Ch'est aën mousse qui sé caomporte bian. I'n beit pas, ni feume pas, ni prend pas des drogues. Chu barboue-là se rensi caonte la muraïle d'la bànque pour lé lessier passaïr. Ch't'assaeure qu'il allait pus qué trente chinq milles par haeure pour s'écappaïr!"

☛

4

A little tale
by Marie De Garis

One afternoon Judy decided to pay a visit to Rachel. They had been friends for more than fifty years, since they began going to the little school at Les Buttes on the same day. There was some fine drizzle, but it was nothing much. Rachel was very pleased to see her and the two of them sat down on the "green-bed" to knit. Judy had taken her sock as usual and Rachel was making a Guernsey for her husband. The needles worked as hard as their tongues when they told each other the latest news in the parish.

Rachel got up to make some tea. While pouring a cup for Judy she said to her, "Listen, I must tell you what happened the other evening just before dark to the nephew of my brother-in-law. He was on his motor-bike along the Vazon road and do you know what he saw? A bogey-man!"

"Oh surely not," said Judy. "A bogey-man? What sort of bogey-man? I didn't think that there was anything like that in Guernsey anymore. Tell me all about it."

"The beast he saw was twice as big as the biggest dog. It had long pointed ears like horns. And the animal walked only on its hind legs and had eyes like saucers."

"Do you think that he had had a drop too much, or had smoked some drug and he was dreaming?" said Judy.

"No," replied Rachel. "He's a lad who behaves properly. He doesn't drink, he doesn't smoke and he doesn't take drugs. That bogey-man moved out of the way against the wall to let him pass. I can assure you that he was going at more than thirty-five miles an hour to escape."

☛

"Gâche-à-pànne," s'fit la Judie. "J'en terfie mé! Tchi qu'nou-s- ôras perchôin?"

V'là les daeux faummes à palaïr atour les r'v'énànts et toutes sortes dé sorcheul'rie et ditaï tché, en buvànt leurs thée. Ils'taient d'avis qué y avait bian tché qui s'passait au jour d'ogniet qui n'pouvait pas ête expllitchi.

"Enfin," s'fit la Judie, en roulànt sa caouche et pitchet ses aidjules à travaers," il y est temps qué j'mé ramasse, les jours saont si court."

"Ah, ch'est les bas jours d'vànt noué," dis la Rachael, "toute mesme, j'sis bian fière qué t'es v'nue passaïr enn'haeure ou daeux."

Ils aeurent aën chocque à quànd al'ouvrissi l'hus, dja, la breune avait épaissi tànt qué nous n'pouvait pas quâsi veis sa môin au d'vànt d'sé.

"Oh mais, Judie, tchi qu'tu t'en vas faire? Tu peux allaïr. Tu té perdéras," dis la Rachael.

"Noufait," répounni la Judie, "j'pourais mé trouvaï pour à la maisaon dauve mes daeux iaers cllos. I faut qué j'aouche préparaïr lé soupaïr. Eibram a la douzôine* à ces sé. La breune sé cllergira p'tête."

La v'là en a arroute. Mais ch'tait épaissier qué l'enfaëuqu'ment faisait. Ch'tait tànt mux qu'a counnissait son ch'min, pasqué oprès qu'all'avait passaïr l'éghise et rentrï dans les p'tites rues pour ciz ielle, a'n veyait goute.

Tout d'aën caoup a ôuit derrière ielle tchique chaose qu'allait "Cllànk, cllànk." Toute intchiette, all'arreti et criyit, "Tchi qu'est là?" Pas d'répaonse, mais la cllànk'rie arretit. Ch'tait pière, pasqué a pouvait ôuit aureun, des grounn'ries et des grànds soupirs, qui la gênais acore pusse.

☛

"Good gracious," said Judy. "I'm terrified. What will we hear of next?"

There were the two women talking about ghosts and all sorts of witchcraft and such things while drinking their tea. They were of the opinion that there were many things which happened these days which couldn't be explained.

"Well," said Judy, rolling up her sock and poking the needles through it, "It's time that I went home, the days are so short."

"Ah, it's the dismal days before Christmas," said Rachel, "all the same I'm very glad that you have come to pass an hour or two."

They had a shock when they opened the door though, the fog had thickened so much that they could hardly see their hands in front of them.

"Oh Judy, what are you going to do? You can't go. You'll get lost," said Rachel.

"No," replied Judy, "I could find my way home with both my eyes closed. I must go and prepare our supper. Abraham has a douzaine meeting tonight. Perhaps the fog will clear."

Off she went on her way. But the mist was getting much thicker. It was just as well that she knew her way because, after she had passed the church and entered the narrow lanes to her house, she couldn't see a thing

Suddenly she heard behind her something which went "Clank, clank." Very nervous, she stopped and called, "Who's there?" No reply, but the clanking stopped. It was worse, because she could hear instead, groaning and great sighs, which frightened her even more.

Par aucht'haeure, bian éffraï, la Judie hâti ses pids. Et derchier "Cllànque, cllànque." All'éprouvit à cours, mais l'artritis dans ses genouaïx l'empêchait d'allaïr vite. Et tout lé temps all'oyait "Cllànque, cllànque." Tout lé d'vis qu'il'avaient iaeux, la Rachael et ielle, y vint pour l'effraïr acore pus. All'tait saeure qué y avait tchique barboue derrière ielle étout. Son tcheur en avait dé étoupaïr la gorge. Et tout lé temps chutte cllànqu'rie-là la sièvait.

Enfin, all'appeurchi ciz-ielle. Et y avait l'Eibram à la haerche. La Judie couoru dans ses bras.

"Oh Eibram, Eibram, y aën barbou souvent mé! Sauve-mé!"

"Aën barboue?" s'fit s'n haomme, chotchit dé veies sa chière p'tite faume dans l'état qu'all'tait.

"Oué, l'ôt-tu?" dit la Judie. Et en veritaï nou-s-oyait tchi qu'était là allaïr acore "Cllànk, cllànk." Eibram prins aën pas enviaer lé camas.

"Eibram, méfie-té," s'écriyit la Judie, effraie pour s'n haomme.

Li, i s'mit à s'bouffaïr à rire.

"Aën barboue!" s'ti. "Vraiment Judie, ton barboue n'est qué la vieille Rosie, la vacque dé not'vaisin, Mess Le Page. I v'nait d'mé téléphonaïr qu'a s'était défitchie d'sa terraïe dans lé praï et si j'y aigu'rais à la trachier. Ch'est-là tchique j'm'en allais justement faire. Ch'tait son pesçaön** qu't'ôyais trônaï sus la rue derrière té!."

By now really terrified, Judy hastened her steps. And again "Clank, clank." She tried to run, but the arthritis in her knees prevented her from going quickly. And all the time she heard "Clank, clank." All the tales which she and Rachel had told each other came back to frighten her even more. She was sure that there was a bogey-man behind her as well. Her heart was in her mouth. And all the time that clanking followed her.

At last she was almost home. And there was Abraham at the gate. Judy ran into his arms.

"Oh Abraham, Abraham, there's a bogey-man after me. Save me!"

"A bogey-man?" said her husband, shocked to see his dear little wife in such a state.

"Yes, do you hear it?" said Judy. And indeed they could hear what was there still going "Clank, clank." Abraham took a step towards the noise.

"Abraham, be careful," cried Judy, afraid for her husband.

He burst out laughing

"A bogey-man!" he said. "Honestly Judy, your bogey-man is only old Rosie, our neighbour, Mr Le Page's cow. He has just telephoned me to say that she has broken loose from where she was grazing in the meadow and would I help him look for her. That's what I was just going to do. It was her iron peg that you could hear dragging on the road behind you!"

---

* Douzaine: Parish Council consisting of a Dean (Chairman) and twelve douzeniers elected by the parish.

** Cows were staked out in the fields and moved twice a day to save grazing.

Enne p'tite sornaette
par Marie De Garis

Le Henri et la Priscille s'enter hàntaient ensemble. Tous les desmanches, en sortànt d'l'éghise les v'là, bras-d'sus, bras-sous, à faire aen p'tit tour. I faisaient aen biau p'tit couplle. Mais y'avait tchinze aens qu'ils allaient d'mesme. Le Henri était aen tràntchille gaillard, bouan travaillaeux, mais jomais avait grand chose à dire. La paure Priscille veyait tous ses vieilles filles dé compognie dauve leurs fomilles à gràndir autour dé iaeux, tandis qu'alle'tait acore vieille fille.

Enfin, aen bouan jour a vit sus lé Press qué ch'tait l'onnaïe bisectille ouecque le 29 février ch'tait lé privilège dé enne faumme à proposaïr mariage. A pensi, "Ch'est ma chance, coute qui coute, chu caoup ou jomais."

J'peux pas vous dire tchi qui s'arrivi, mais tout chi qué j'sais, ch'est qué lé perchôin samedi i'furent à la ville, les daeux, accataïr la bague d'engagement. Et à Pâques y'avait des gràànds neuches à l'éghise, dauve lé chant et les clloques qui tinçardais bouan frais à quànd i'sortaient dé la porte dé l'éghise.

A little yarn
by Marie De Garis

Henry and Priscilla kept company together. Every Sunday, on coming out of church, there they were, arm in arm, off on a little walk. They made a lovely couple. But they had been doing that for fifteen years. Henry was a quiet chap, a good worker, who never had much to say. Poor Priscilla saw all her old girl friends with their families growing up around them, while she was still an old maid.

At last, one fine day, she saw on the Press that it was Leap Year, when on February 29 it was the woman's privilege to propose marriage. She thought, "It's my chance, come what may, this time or never."

I can't tell you what happened, but all that I know, is that the next Saturday they went to Town, the two of them, to buy the engagement ring. And at Easter there was a great wedding at the church, with the choir and the bells ringing out heartily when they came out of the church door.

La Julie et la Princesse
par Marie de Garis

I s'en allais aver enn'électiaon pour députaï dans la paraesse, et nous oyait les ardjuments pour et caonte les daeux candidats déjà noumaïs.

"Oprès tout," s'fit la Marguerite à la Julie, "nous devrai en aver aen bouan pour les chinq milles livres sterlin qu'i r'chève pour ête dans l's Etats."

"Chinq milles livres sterlin!" répouni la Julie. "Je n'savais pas qu'il'tais payi comme chena, mé. Cor, chinq milles livres sterlin! J'm'en vais d'mandaïr à Eibram de s'maette candidat. J'cré qu'en haomme comme li, qu'est bian counnaeux et respectaï, et aen douzinier décaoute, érai enne bouanne chànce d'ête élu."

La v'là daonc, chutte serraïe-là, quànd il'tais au lliet, tràntchille et tout caoud, qui dit, "O-tu Eibram, sais-tu qu'aen députaï est payi chinq milles livres sterlin pour ête dans l's Etats?"

Eibram était quasi endormi, et i n'la répounit pas, sinaon baillier et aen "Hum....hum."

"Ecoute, Eibram. Tu pourrai ête députaï, té. Pense à tchique nous pourrai faire dauve ches sous-là. Nous pourrai mesme allaïr pour aen "cruise" au tour du maonde. Et tu sais, Eibram, tu f'rai justement aen bouan députaï."

L'Eibram s'assievi drat dans l'lliet.

"Esche troubllaïe qué t'es?" i d'mandi à sa faumme. "Si tu trache aën députaï dans chutte fomille, met-té té-mesme. Je n'veur pas ouït daoute d'chu gniolin-là."

Et l'Eibram s'couchi derchier, le daos à ielle et dans p'tit d'temps, raonflliai comme aen viar boeu, mais la Julie resti laongtemps évilli.

6

Julie and the Princess
by Marie de Garis

There was going to be an election for deputy* in the parish, and we heard the arguments for and against the two candidates already named.

"After all," said Marguerite to Julie, " we should have a good one for the five thousand pounds that they receive for being in the States."

"Five thousand pounds!" replied Julie. "I didn't know that they were paid like that, me! Cor, five thousand pounds! I'm going to ask Abraham to stand as a candidate. I think that a man like him, who is well known and respected, and a douzenier (parish official) as well, would have a good chance of being elected."

So there she was, that evening, when they were in bed, quiet and nice and warm, saying, "I say, Abraham, do you know that a deputy is paid five thousand pounds for being in the States?"

Abraham was almost asleep, and he didn't answer her except for yawning and saying, "Hum...hum.."

"Listen, Abraham. You, you could be a deputy. Think of what we could do with that money. We could even go on a cruise around the world. And you know, Abraham, you would make a really good deputy."

Abraham sat up straight in bed.

"Are you mad?" he asked his wife. "If you are looking for a deputy in this family, put yourself forward. I don't want to hear another word about this twaddle."

And Abraham lay down again, with his back to her and, in a short time, was snoring like an old bull, but Julie stayed awake a long time.

☛

"Hum," a pensit, "v'là enn'idée. J'en parl'rai à la Marguerite."

La Marguerite était d'accord d'la proposaï et v'là la Julie ieune des candidats. A l'Assembllaïe d'Parraesse d'vànt l'électiaon, all'tait dauve les daeux autes candidats et l'counétablle qu'était dans la tchaire, à ête tchestounaï par les électeurs atour tchiqu'i f'rais s'il'tais élus.

Si vous avaites ouit la Julie! Mesme Eibram fut surpris et orgillaeux d'ses répaonses. A fit si bian qué, à l'électiaon, les daeux autes candidates n'aurent pas quasi d'votes sinaon les sians de laeux fomilles.

Et v'là la Julie dans l's Etats. A pernais la parole chaque caoup que les Etats étais assembllaï. A pouvais faire aen "speech", j'vous assaeure. A gogniais son pouint terrous et all'tait su enamas d'coumités étou!

Aen jour, le Bailiff voulait l'y parlaïr.

"Julie," dit le Bailiff – i la counnisait enamas bian par aucht'haeure – "Julie, la Princesse s'en viant en Guernési perchoin meis. Mon coumité oimrait que tu l'i persent'rais le touffé d'flleurs à enne réceptiaon à Beau Séjour."

Créyous qu'la Julie était fière et orgillaeuse étou. A pensit, "I'm faut aen neut froc, aen chapé, des gànts et des sôlers à hauts talaons. Tout à la drôine mode. Ma picture det ête dans l'"Praesse" oprès tout."

Comme a die, "Aucht'haeure que j'gogne chinq milles livres sterlin, j'peu m'affordaï d'aver des bouannes hardes pour l'occasiaon. A fus à la ville et all' acatis aen biau froc d'souaie et tout chu qu'il'y fallait – et des sôlers à hauts talaons.

Quànd a mourtit tout chu qu'all'avait acataï à Eibram, tout fut bian au prumier. Mais quànd i vit les sôlers, i die, "Absolument, tu t'en va pas t'mourtaï atour des sôlers d'mesme!"

"Pourtchi pas," répounit-alle. "des sôlers d'mesme saont d'la drôine mode."

"Hum," she thought, "that's an idea. I'll talk about it to Marguerite."

Marguerite agreed to propose her and so Julie was one of the candidates. At the Parish Assembly before the election, she was with the other two candidates and the constable who was in the chair, being questioned by the electors about what they would do if they were elected.

If you had heard Julie! Even Abraham was surprised and proud of her answers. She did so well that, at the election, the two other candidates had hardly any votes apart from those of their families.

And so there was Julie in the States. She spoke each time that the States was assembled. She could make a speech, I can assure you. She always won her point and she was on a lot of committees as well.

One day, the Bailiff wanted to speak to her.

"Julie," said the Bailiff – he knew her well by now – " Julie, the Princess is coming to Guernsey next month. My committee would like you to present the bouquet to her at a reception at Beau Séjour."

Don't you think that Julie was pleased and proud too. She thought, "I need a new dress, a hat, some gloves and some high-heeled shoes. All in the latest fashion. My picture should be in the "Press" after all."

As she said, "Now that I'm earning five thousand pounds, I can afford to have the best clothes for the occasion." She went to town and she bought a lovely silk dress and all that she needed – and some high-heeled shoes.

When she showed all that she had bought to Abraham, everything went well at first. However, when he saw the shoes, he said, "Surely, you're not going to show yourself in shoes like that!"

"Why not," she replied," shoes like these are in the latest fashion."

☛

Et bian, nous est des gens respectabll, et j'en m'en vais pas répetar chu qu'i l'y dit. Eibram pouvais ête raide pllat en des temps. Tous les caoups qu'il rentri à la maisaon, a l'y fit aen "curtsey".

"Cor chapin," s'fit Eibram aen caoup, "tu n'm'a jomais mourtaï tànt d'respet d'vànt.

Enfin, v'là le grand jour qu'arrive. Toute la nobllaessse de Guernési était assembllaï à Beau Séjour. La Julie parraisai bian, mais a n'tait pas accoutumaï à si hauts talaons. Quànd le Bailiff l'i fit l'saegne, la Julie s'appeurchis d'la Princaesse.

Et pis, malheur! En faisànt son "curtsey", la Julie twistit son colet d'pid su ses hauts talaons! Pour se sauvaïr, a saisis le froc de la Princaesse. La paure Princaesse éprouuvis à s'gardaïr de d'but. Les v'là les daeux gav'laïes; les daeux tchulbutaïes en l'aer. Oh!Le tripot!

L'affaire s'fit si vite et tous les gens là fures si chotchi, que n'iauex pas aen mot d'dit. La paure Julie n'osais pas ouvri les iaers!

Et pis, a ouit la vouaix d'Eibram, "Tchi qu'tu cré qu't'es à faire hors du lliet? T'as toutes les couvertures autour de té. Tu saonge."

Oprès tchiques minutes, la Julie r'vint à ielle-mesme. I n'y avait pas d'princaesse, ni Bailiff, – persaonne. Riocque l'Eibram! All'tais dans sa chambre. Eibram se plliogniait qu'il 'tait g'laï d'fré sans ses couvertures. All'avait saongi tout!

J'peux vous dire que son naom n'fus pas mit su la liste de candidats pour députaï. Comme a dit à la Marguerite le lànd'moin quànd a l'y caontit la déjonie, "Quànd mesme qu'i m'pay'rais chent milles livres sterlin, j'en voudrais pas m'y matte! Nennin djà!"

Well, we are respectable people, and I am not going to repeat what he said. Abraham could be very coarse sometimes. Every time he came home, she would make him a curtsey.

"Good gracious," said Abraham once, "you have never shown me so much respect before."

At last the great day came. All the great and good of Guernsey were assembled at Beau Séjour. Julie looked well, but she wasn't used to such high-heeled shoes. When the Bailiff gave her the sign, Julie approached the Princess.

And then, good heavens! Whilst making her curtsey, Julie twisted her ankle on her high-heels! To save herself, she seized the Princess's dress. The poor Princess tried to stay upright. The two of them fell headlong, both of them upside down. Oh! What a to-do!

It happened so quickly and all the people there were so shocked, that not a word was said. Poor Julie didn't dare open her eyes.

And then she heard Abraham's voice, "What do you think you are doing out of bed? You've got all the bed-clothes around you. You're dreaming."

After a few minutes, Julie came to her senses. There was no Princess nor Bailiff, – no-one. Only Abraham! She was in her bed room. Abraham was complaining that he was freezing without his covers. She had dreamed everything.

I can tell you that her name was not put forward on the list of candidates for deputy. As she said to Marguerite the next day when she told her the whole rigmarole, "Even though they paid me a hundred thousand pounds, I wouldn't want to be one! No fear!"

★ Deputy: an elected representative in the States of Deliberation – the island parliament.

Le neut chapé
par Marie De Garis

Ch'tait l'Anniversaire lé perchôin desmanche et la p'tite Alice avait aen neut chapé d'paille à bllu ribans qui pendaient en derrière. Al'en caontait tché d'son chapé.

Lé samedi arlévaïe sa mere s'en fut pour la ville. La Lizzie vint l'y criaïr pour allaïr à la bogniolle dauve ielle. L'Alice, chutte p'tite fou-là, mit sen neut chapé et s'en fut daonc pour la bànque.

Les daeux filles sé dégriyirent et mis laeux hardes à n'aen p'tit mouchet sus la bànque et lé chapé d'l'Alice en d'sus.

Mais la maïr était sus lé montànt et à quànd i sortirent dé iaoux laeux hardes étaient à fllo. I réussirent à les sauvaïs, mais lé biau chapé à bllu ribans était déjà bian llian, sus l'ch'min pour l'Amerique.

J'm'en vais pas vous dire tchique sa mere l'y dis, et l'y fis, mais lé laond'môin a fut oblligi dé récitaï sa piaeche à l'Anniversaire dauve aen viar chape d'hivaer sus sa tête.

The new hat
by Marie De Garis

It was the Anniversary* next Sunday and little Alice had a new straw hat with blue ribbons which hung down behind. She was very proud of her hat.

On Saturday afternoon her mother went to town. Lizzie came to call for her to go for a swim with her. Alice, that little fool, put on her new hat and went off to the beach.

The two girls undressed and put their clothes in a little pile and Alice's hat on top.

But the sea was rising and when they came out of the water, their clothes were afloat. They succeeded in saving them , but the lovely hat with blue ribbons was already far away, well on the way to America.

I'm not going to tell you what her mother said to her, or what she did to her, but the next day she was obliged to recite her piece at the Anniversary with an old winter hat on her head.

---

* Anniversary: Yearly celebration of the foundation of a Methodist Sunday School when everyone wore new clothes and the children performed recitations etc.

Au haut du gardin
par Nellie Duquemin

Au haut des notre gardin y a en petit maisaon. A la deux pllaich dauve trais pertu: a grand, a moyen et a petit. Aux sers devat la nieght, mum dit, "Via-ann garcaons, allai au gardin devat la nieght, et prenez votre petit frere. Chez bian vite votre soupai."

Whek es le petit? Ils nous a dit que il ete stichee. Il es acore la.

"Va le trachiai. T'es ma fille. Chez garcaons aon pas d'idee!"

Eh bian, i'n pouvais pas sortir dai d'la. Cas les gras sort fur, les places etais fremes. Et vere le petit dit;

"Ma chemise et tout etreie."

At the top of the garden
by Nellie Duquemin

At the top of our garden there is a privy. There are two places with three holes; a large one, a middle-sized one and a small one. In the evening before nightfall, Mum said, "Now then boys, go up the garden before dark and take your little brother with you. It will soon be supper-time."

Where is the little one? They told us that he was stuck. He's still there.

"Go and find him. You're my daughter. These boys have no idea!"

Well, he couldn't get out of there. When the older ones went, the places were closed. And the little one said:

"My shirt is all torn."

La bounne gache (Enne vraie histouaire)
par Nellie Duquemin

Les droin Noue dai l'Otchupation, eh bien par gras choase pour Noue. Ma soeur mai dit, "Ton papier la aupres ta fnete, il est triste."

"Sait bien, mais jen menvais pas fer servi ma fieur pour chenna."

"Ah tu acore du papier? J'ai des chet qui fras pour chenna. Cas ta fille vas a la ville Samedi pour trouvai la Mary dauve la grape jai stiet pour tai a nous faire des petite gaches pour Noue, jlai metrai etou dauve le traffic pour ramondai."

Eh bien, le Samedi vin et jhalli les pepins d'la grape, et jla coupi en morceaux pour la faire put petit, mais jen sai pas des petit jaune. Jnai shomais veux chenna dans ma vie, mais crais chez d'la poudre oueque a tais jaune. Eh bien, i faut la faire en poudre pour la mette dans la gache dauve le martai, et envlopais dans en chic, mai a la batte. Eh bien, en effort, mais je fait mes petit gache ils tai belle est jaune.

Aupres Noue cas ma soeur vin, eh bien, "Les gaches etais bounne a Noue."

"Manifique, mais tu nas pas ramondais ton papier acore."

"Nan, cie arretez pour quaique tu allez monvias."

"Mais ils tai dauve le trafi dai Noue!"

Chu jaune la, mais il fut dans la gache. Mais chette dlopais pour les courtains comme nous faisai servi. Nous pourais tout ete morts.

Good cake (A true story)
by Nellie Duquemin

The last Christmas of the Occupation, well there wasn't much around for Christmas. My sister said to me, "Your wallpaper there by the window, it looks terrible."

"I know, but I'm not using my flour* for that."

"Have you got any more paper? I've got something to fix that. When your daughter goes to Town on Saturday to meet Mary with the grapes I've dried for you to make a little cake for Christmas, I'll put it in with the stuff to mend it."

Well, Saturday came and I took the pips out of the grapes and I cut them in pieces to make them smaller, but I didn't know what the little yellow things were. I had never seen anything like that in my life, but I thought that it was powder where they (the grapes) were yellow. Well, I had to turn them into powder to put in the cake with a hammer, they were wrapped in a cloth with me hitting them. Well, it was an effort, I made my little cakes and they were lovely and yellow.

After Christmas, when my sister came, well, " The cakes were good at Christmas."

"Lovely, but you haven't mended your wallpaper."

"No, I've been waiting until you sent the stuff to me."

" But it was with the things for Christmas!"

That yellow stuff, it went into the cake. It was starch for the curtains like we used to use. We could all have died!

---

* Wallpaper paste was made with flour and water at that time.

Les sale jenyaux
par Nellie Duquemin

Aupres la guerre ma soeur Mabel Poat et son petit garcon David dmeuraint a l'Hotel de France et ma soeur fut "warden" pour les Etats, et les gens qui navez pas du cheboan allez la. Eh bien, ils la mir dans an petit cottage aupres l'hotel mais il nettez pas gramont nait.

"Vien majais a le r'parai," am'die et jfut scrubai et a la fin il'tai mue. A quatre heures jmi ramassi vite pour la boss pour Cobo.

Assise dans la boss, jpensi vais dans lmirreaux aupres le cacheur des nair jenyaux. Cor shapan, jpensi, yon vla une dauve des fichu sale jenyaux. Et bien, ma fee, ches les mions! Jmis vite mon frau par desus. La Bassasse!

Dirty knees
by Nellie Duquemin

After the war my sister Mabel Poat and her little boy lived at the Hotel de France and my sister was "warden" for the States, and people who didn't have any coal went there. Well, they moved her into a little cottage next to the hotel but it wasn't very clean.

"Come and help me clean it," she said and I went to scrub it and at last it was better. At four o'clock I went quickly to get the bus for Cobo.

Sitting in the bus, I thought I could see in the mirror by the driver some black knees. Good heavens, I thought, there's a woman with some awfully dirty knees.

Well, s'truth, they're mine! I quickly pulled my dress over them. The shame of it!

L'expérience de la Nellie
par Nellie Duquemin

Quand jettez en petite fille ya pus d'chinquant ans, ma mere mai dissez, "A 'sa r'iven vite de l'ecole, car il faut que t'al en course pour ta soeur."

Ma soeur etais en veuve; a faissez du lavain pour les messius pour vive, et pour payer lais docture pasque a l'avez a petit garcon qui etais terjous malade.

Eh bien, mai pernez le lange tous naite est maison, et j'rammasie le sal sur en pour vielle bike. V'la qu'etais bien, mais fallez que j'futs a Ste. Helene. Chettez pas aen cabaret en chu temps la.

I'yavez des grand arbes fras a l'hus de derriere, nous veies cas ni chen. La daume qui demurais la se leve riocque durant la gniet, et j'la croinee comme le faëu.

J'etais chet mort de peus, j'marchi tous doucement amaön le chemin, les bouchette qui cracheai sous mes pids mai effrai. J'ouvrais l'hus tous doucement, mettez le naite baloe bas, et rammaseai le sal, et aussi vite comme mes gabbes pouvez me portai, j'montai su mon bike et j'nais pas en derriere devant d'etre est Vauxbelets.

Yas t il aux cheun autre qu'il craine chique chose q'il nans jamais veus?

11

Nellie's experience
by Nellie Duquemin

When I was a little girl more than fifty years ago, my mother used to say to me, "Now then come back quickly from school because you must go on an errand for your sister."

My sister was a widow; she did the washing for the gentry in order to live, and to pay the doctors because she had a little boy who was always ill.

Well, I took the clean linen to the houses, and I collected the dirty linen on my poor old bike. That was alright, but I had to go to Ste. Helene. It was not a public house at that time.

There were some big trees right up to the back door, there was not a cat or dog to be seen. The lady who lived there only got up during the night, and I was terrified of her.

I was half dead with fright, I walked very quietly up the path, the twigs cracking under my feet frightening me. I opened the door very slowly, put the clean bundle down, and collected the dirty one, and as quickly as my legs could carry me, I got on my bike and I didn't look behind me before reaching the Vauxbelets.

Is there anyone else who is frightened of something they have never seen?

12

La vaque de Nico
par P J Girard

L'p'tit Nico, au contraire d'la majoritaï des ignorants, avait graend respect pour l'education – pernaïz couontise que j'écris "avait" parce que l'experience dauve sa vaque l'y changit entièrement s'n opinion.

Ch'tait Moussieu Le Grand, bouan houme qui l'"tait, qui commenchit l'affaire quand i prêtit des vieilles copies du *Farmer's Weekly* a son vaisin, le p'tit Nico, qui s'mit brâmant a passair ses serraies a les llière. Il était interessi dans toutes les articles, écrites autour le fermage, supareilment s'il étaient écrites par tchi graend professseur.

Dans ieune de ches articles ichin, i lut daonc que des vaques traites au son d'la musique dounnaient bien pus d'laite que les ciennes traites à la vieille monière.

Nico pensit otcher qu'd'en avair mal à la tête, et à la fin i décidit de faire enne épreuvre su sa vieille vaque qui v'nait d'vêlair mais qui dounnait qu'aen pot d'laite par traite.

Le bouan jour vint, tout était prêt; le temps pour traire etait v'nu, le bande était arrivai et toute la contraie était assembiae (sans en être priaie) dans l'belle d'la ferme de Nico. Dans l'bas du belle, y avait fiquie enne baite, graende, maigre et fichument laide qu'était supposaie d'être enne vaque.

Nico était entièrement excitai et quaend l'houme atou le gros tambour li d'mandit si voulait le "Twist" ou le "Bougi-Wougi", i n'savait pas qui mal pauretai qui fallait dire.

A la fin tout était prêt et Nico, équippai atou aen biau bieu d'vanté amarrai dauve aen bieanc taquet et enne canne entre ses genouias, s'assiévit su aen scabé sous la vaque et bayit aen sine pour que le bande qu'menchisse.

☞

Nico's cow
by P J Girard

Little Nico, contrary to the majority of ignorant people, had great respect for education – take notice that I write "had" because the experience with his cow changed his opinion entirely.

It was Mr Le Grand, good man that he was, who began the affair when he lent old copies of the *Farmer's Weekly* to his neighbour, little Nico, who immediately began to pass his evenings reading them. He was interested in all the articles written about farming, especially if they were written by a well-known professor.

In one of these articles, he read that cows milked to the sound of music gave much more milk than those milked in the old way.

Nico thought until he had a headache, and at last he decided to have a trial run on his old cow that had just calved but only gave a pot* of milk each milking.

The great day came, everything was ready; the time for milking came, the band had arrived and all the district had assembled (without being invited) in Nico's farmyard. At the bottom of the yard, there was staked an animal, big, thin and terribly ugly that was supposed to be a cow.

Nico was really excited and when the man with the big drum asked him if he wanted the "Twist" or the "Boogie-Woogie" he didn't know what on earth to say.

At last everything was ready and Nico equipped with a lovely white apron tied with a white tape and a milk-can between his knees, sat down on a milking stool under the cow and gave the sign for the band to begin.

Mais, maleur de maleur-sabér de bouais, à la prumière barre de musique, la vieille mourtit pus d'vie qu'a n'avait jomais fait, dans ses dix-huit ans, car a l'vit la tête, fit aen pas en d'vant et pis dauve aen brait l'vit les deaux guérets d'derrière, cotpie Nico les quinsbourgs en haut dans la varvaquière et fichit l'camp avos l'gardin.

J'vous dis ch'est que ch'tait triste, les gens éraient deu braire mais j'ai haonte de vous dire l'piesi les print et tous s'mirent à rire comme des perdus.

Nico s'ramassit d'dans la varvaquière atou sa bouanne parre de brais de ticsette toute ruinaie, et il entrit en d'dans. Si l'bande créyait qu'il'tait parti queure leux guinés i furent bien trompais quaend Nico sortit atou enne grosse arme à deaux baris.

J'vous d'mande si les gens s'ramassirent amont la cache, ch'tait comme si le diable d'enfer avait étai souvent de iaeux.

L'p'tit Nico, sa furie passaie, en r'gardant la vieille qui mangeait treanquill'ment dans l'gardin, dit, "Ma fai, j'pense que ch'est miyau marchi de traire enne vieille vaque que d'éprouvair à la faire dounnair pus d'laite suivant les épreuves de fous qui n'y counnisent vert ni gris."

Et ch'est daonc comme chena que la vaque de Nico l'fit joindre la majoritai des ignorants à condannair l'education.

But good gracious, heavens above, at the first bar of music the old girl showed more life than she had ever done in her eighteen years, for she raised her head, took a step forward and then with a bellow she lifted her two back legs and kicked Nico head over heels into the slime-pit and cleared off down the garden.

I can tell you that it was a sorry sight, the people should have wept, but I'm ashamed to say that they were overcome with mirth and everyone began to laugh heartily.

Nico got out of the slime-pit with his good pair of corduroy trousers completely ruined, and went inside. If the band thought that he had gone fetch their money they were sadly mistaken when Nico came out with a big double-barrelled gun.

I ask you if the people cleared off up the yard; it was as if the the devil had been after them.

Little Nico, his fury gone, and looking at the old girl who was quietly eating in the garden, said, "S'truth, I think that it's cheaper to milk an old cow than to try to make her give more milk by following the advice of the fools who know nothing at all about it."

And so that is how Nico's cow made him join the majority of ignorant people in condemning education.

---

*   Pot: Guernsey measure equal to half a gallon or four pints

13

Enne seraïe au fin d'leune
par Enid Green

Aen bouan jour quànd la Marguerite et Jean Toumas etais assis a la tablle a desnaïr, Jean Toumas mit sen couté et sa fourchaette bas su la tablle et dit, "Pour me j'sie onnaïr de chenchin, ch'est tous les jours du lard."

La Marguerite le r'gardit coume si a n'lé creyait pas, et a lie dit, "Mais ch'est du bouan lard de su les lattes."

"Et bian," si fait Jean Toumas, "j'saï bian q'chest du lard de su les lattes, mais i l'est rouète."

Tout d'aen caoup i dit a la Marguerite, "J'sai tchi q'nous fra, d'moin au saer nous ira dentché les Pesqueries vais si nous era du lanchaön."

Le lendemoin au saer, aupres soupaïr et les vessiaux l'avaïr, v'la Jean Toumas qui mit ses grosses braies de corder-aie, et sa grosse casaque, et sa calotte ensi enfaönsaïe coume i pouvait. V'la la Marguerite qui met sen scoupe, et a mit tànt d'hardes que nous l'erait pas jomais r'counaeuse.

V'la Jean Toumas qui prend la bêque et l'ponier-a cau, et la Marguerite print la lanterne pour en tous cas que la leune s'rait mushie derriere des nouages.

Quànd i l'arivirent est Pesqueries, v'la Jean Toumas qui s'mit a bestché dans l'gravier, mais pas rian du tout a vais, mais i continuit, et tout daën caoup, le v'la excitaïr, et la Marguerite, vive coume enne bellàtte*, attrappe le lànchaon et le met dans ponier-a-cau.

Quànd a r'gardait dans l'ponier, a pensait a tout l'travas q'a s'en allait avait a prepapaïr tout shu lanchaön la, mais daön Jean Toumas c'menchait a ête lassa:ir, qui fait i decidirent de sen allair pour la maisaon.

☛

13

One moonlit evening
by Enid Green

One day when Marguerite and John Thomas were sitting at the table eating their dinner, John Thomas put his knife and fork down on the table and said, "I'm really fed up with this, every day we have fat bacon."

Marguerite looked at him as if she didn't believe him, and she told him, "But it's good bacon from on the bacon rack."

"Well," said John Thomas, "I know that it's bacon from on the rack, but it's rancid."

Suddenly he said to Marguerite, "I know what we'll do, tomorrow evening we'll go as far as the Pesqueries to see if we can get some sand-eels."

The next evening, after supper and the dishes washed, John Thomas put on his heavy corduroy trousers, his old coat, and his cap pulled down as far as he could. Marguerite put on her scoop (Guernsey bonnet), and she put on so many clothes that we would never have recognised her.

John Thomas took his spade and his fish basket, and Marguerite took the lantern in case the moon was hidden behind the clouds.

When they arrived at the Pesqueries, John Thomas began to break up the beach gravel, but there was nothing to be seen, but he carried on and suddenly he became very excited; Marguerite, lively as a stoat, caught the sand-eel and put it in the fish basket.

When she looked in the basket, she thought of all the work that she was going to have to do to prepare all those sand-eels, but then John Thomas began to be tired so they decided to go home.

☛

Le lendemoin, quànd Jean Toumas vint pour sen mie-matin, y avait pas rian a vais. La Marguerite avait gardaïr tout mushit. Mais quànd i vint pour sen desnaïr dauve le naïr en l'aer, i sentait aen bouan gout, et she's q'il tait fiàr.

Aupres qui furent fini desnaïr, en frottànt sa barbe, i dit a la Marguerite, "Et bian Marguerite, shena valait la poine de passaïr sa serraïe est Pesqueries au fin d'leune."

Et coume se fait la Marguerit, "Mais verre Jean Toumas, et j'espere bian q'nous pourra i r'tournaïr l'pershoin fin d'leune."

"Mais oui dja Marguerite nous ira."

Quànd vint le pershoin fin d'leune, v'la la Marguerite et Jean Toumas allaïr pour les Pesqueries vait pour du lanchaön, mais shute seraïe la, y en avait pas iun a vais, qui fait Jean Toumas fût oblligit de s'contentaï dauve du lard q'etait rouête.

---

* bellàtte: A Guernsey idiom for a lively person

Next day, when John Thomas came for his mid-morning break, there was nothing to be seen. Marguerite had kept everything hidden away. But when he came in for his dinner with his nose in the air, he smelled a lovely smell, and wasn't he pleased.

After they had finished their dinner, whilst stroking his beard, he said to Marguerite, "Well, it was worth taking the trouble to spend the evening at the Pesqueries in the moonlight."

As Marguerite said, "Yes, John Thomas, and I hope that we will be able to go back there the next time there is moonlight."

"Of course Marguerite, we'll go."

Next time it was moonlight, Marguerite and John Thomas went to the Pesqueries to look for sand-eels, but there wasn't one to be seen. So John Thomas had to be content with fat bacon that was rancid.

Les Ormars
par T A Grut

Oy'ous, aim'ous l's ormars? Ch'est donc d'quiet bouan quànd i sont bien cuits, mais ch'est qu'i faut saver les trimaï.

I faut les battre dur pour les faire dev'nir molles (justement comme nous battrait les cràgnons quànd i sont d'sobéissànts) et pis les "steweï" ou les fricachier. Je l's aime mues que l'dindon ou l'poulet, biau que ch'n'est qu'à Noué qu'nous en goute.

J'ai grand envie d'une bouanne pllatlaïe d'ormars, caer j'en ai jamais ieüe qu'un caoup d'pis qu'la loué disait qu'i n'fallait poui d'autre allaï en trachier

Men viel hômme, Eliazar, est d'la Chapelle, et n'voulait poui allaï passaï en trachier comme tous les vaisins faisaient. Et quànd i r'venaient d'la bànque, la panraïe était toute couvarte de fyies, pour faire la meine que n'y avait que des fyies.

Unn' seraïe j'alli ciz not' vaisin, Paul Breton, pour vée si i m'invitrait à soupaï, caer j'l'avais rencontreï d'vier très haeures atout sa panraïe d'ormars. Mais quànd j'tappi à l'us, les poures Bretons quâsi mouorirent d'effret, caer i créyaient que ch'tait les "policeman", et que quiqu'un avait délattaï contre le poure Paul.

Quànd j'c'menchi à crieï que ch'tait seulement mé, Nancy Ferbrache, il'ouvrirent l'us et m'invitirent à soupeï d'leux fricot. J'vous as saeure qu'i n'eurent poui à mé d'màndeï le daeuxième caoup, caer j'mouorrais d'envie.

14

The ormers
by T A Grut

Hey, do you like ormers? They are really good when they are well cooked, but you have to know how to prepare them

You must beat them hard to make them soft (just like you would beat the kids when they are disobedient) and then stew them or fry them. I like them better than turkey or chicken; even though we only taste them at Christmas.

I have a great longing for a plateful of ormers because I have only had them once since the law said that we couldn't go and look for them anymore.

My old man, Eleazar, goes to Chapel, and didn't want to go and look for them like all the neighbours did. And when they came back from the beach, the basketful was covered with limpets to make out that there were only limpets in there.

One evening I went to the house of our neighbour, Paul Breton, to see if he would invite me to supper, because I had met him at around three o'clock with his basket of ormers. But when I knocked at the door, the poor Bretons nearly died of fright because they thought that it was the police, and someone had informed against poor Paul.

When I began to call out that it was only me, Nancy Ferbrache, they opened the door and invited me to share in their feast. I can assure you that they didn't have to ask me a second time, for I was dying of envy.

J'n'étais guère de r'tour à la maison, quand Eliâzar r'vint de s'n assembllaïe et était tout prêt pour sen soupaï. J'avais mangi tànt d'ormars ciz les Bretons qui m'était impossible de mangier, et j'eu à dire à m'n hômme que j'avais mal à l'estoma, et que j'creyais que ch'tait la soupe que j'avaimes ieue au méjeu qu'était trop grasse.

Si Eliazar était comme un autre hômme, j'erraimes ieue d's ormars à chaque grànde maraïe, mais nennin, Eliazar a unn'pus delicate conschienche qu'aucheun chréquien, et jamais n'vouli y allaï

Si m'n hômme mouorait, jamais je n'en r'prendrais ïeun qui s'rait Econôme à la Chapelle ou collecteur à l'Egllise; mais Eliazar est fort et robuste comme un ch'và et têtu comme un âne. J'n'errai jamais la chànce de m'en debarassaï, caer i n'mourra jamais d'unn' mort naturelle, et mon seul espoir est qu'la "bosse" qui va pour Plleinmont l'assoum'ra quique serraïe.

D'vant que d'acceptaï un daeuxième hômme, je l'frais promettre d'avanche qui'i m'obéirai terjôus et ira ès ormars quànd le l'i d'màndrai, pour que j'errais men fricot.

Ch'est "alright" de faire unn'loué si tous la garde, mais je n'aïme poui à passaï les maisons ouêque i sont à les fricachier et que ma share s'ra seulement à sentir et poui gouteï

J'espère qu'men perchain hômme s'ra un policeman, et pis'i n'erra poui à allaï ès ormars, mais il erra à prendre les paniers de cheux qui y ont etaï; et n'erra qu'à s'muchier derrière la brecque d'la bànque, et pourra gardaïr ses pids et ses brées sec.

I had only just returned home when Eleazar came back from the meeting and was ready for his supper. I had eaten so many ormers at the Bretons' house that it was impossible for me to eat anything, and I had to tell my husband that I had stomach-ache, and that I thought that the soup which we had had at midday had been too greasy.

If Eleazar had been like other men, we would have had ormers at each spring tide, but no, Eleazar had a more delicate conscience than any Christian, and never would go there ormering.

If my husband died, I would never have another one who was a steward at Chapel or a sidesman in Church; but Eleazar is as strong and robust as a horse and obstinate as a donkey. I will never have the chance to get rid of him, for he will never die a natural death, and my only hope is that the bus which goes to Pleinmont will knock him down one evening.

Before accepting second husband, I would make him promise in advance that he would always obey me and would go ormering when I asked him to, so that I could have my feast.

It's alright to make a law if everyone keeps it, but I don't like to pass houses where they are frying them, and my share will be only to smell them and not to taste them.

I hope that my next husband will be a policeman, and then he won't have to go ormering, but he will have to take the baskets from those who have been there; and he will only have to hide behind the entrance to the beach, and he will be able to keep his feet and trousers dry.

Les T'chens
par T A Grut

Guernesi en bouit! J'voudrais que les charcutiers s'mettraient à l's attrapaï, unn' vingtaine à la fais, pour en faire des sauchisses; j'espère qu'i vêront ma lettre et s'mettront au job tout d'suite, et la Communautaï en s'rait bien r'counnisànt, caer n'y errait poui tànt d'chens par les rues, et les peaures erraient leux sauchisses à bouan marchi. J'en ai jamais gouteï, mais j'cré qu'i s'raient bouannes et un change, caer les Docteurs disent qu'un change de nourriture est bouan pour la santaï.

I y a assai d'chens en Guernesi pour nous dounneï des sauchisses pour quique' annaïes, et pis nous pourrait marchier par les rues sans dangier d'être culbutteï par mettre le pid dans leux salteï, ou d'être échippeï de d'sus sen "bike" quànd les t'chens sont à joueï ou querelleï par les rues.

I y a un aute chose: n'y errait poui d'bracterie par jeur ni d'niet, à distorbeï les gens. Nous pourrait dormir toute la niet comme des nouviaux nais. Lè dangier dans les rues est terriblle, atou les motos, les "bikes"et les t'chens. Les effàns et les vieilles gens ont unn' bouanne chance de termineï leux cârrière d'avànche; et après tout, tous ont l'dérouet d'vivre ensi longtemps comme i pourront.

Je seigne men nom d'fille
Betsi Chen
des Chens, à Tortevà

P.S. Quand les charcutiers erraot fini des t'chens, I pourront c'menchier su les cats, et les sauchisses errot l'gôut d'lapi.

Dogs
by T A Grut

Guernsey is full of them! I wish that the cooked meat butchers would go out and catch them, twenty at a time, to make sausages of them; I hope that they will see my letter and will get on with the job straight away, and the Community would be very grateful, because there would not be so many dogs on the roads, and the poor would have their sausages very cheaply. I have never tasted them, but I think that they would be good and a change, because Doctors say that a change is good for the health.

There are enough dogs in Guernsey to give us sausages for a few years, and we would be able to walk the streets without fear of falling over by putting a foot in their mess, or being knocked off our bike when the dogs are playing or quarrelling in the streets.

There's another thing; there would be no barking day and night, to disturb the people. We would be able to sleep all night like newborn babies. The danger in the streets is terrible, with all the motor-bikes, the bikes and the dogs. Children and old people have a good chance of ending their career prematurely; and after all, everyone has the right to live as long as they can.

I sign my maiden name
Betsy Jehan
Les Jehans, Torteval

P. S. When the cooked meat butchers have finished the dogs, they can start on the cats, and the sausages will taste of rabbit.

16

V'la Noué qu'appeurche
par TA Grut

Comme le temps s'pâsse donc vite! I'msemblle que n'y a qu'un an ou daeux que mon frère et mé pendaimes nos caûches au pid du llièt pour être empllies par le "Sandy Claws" qui d'vallait par la chimnaïe, et ochetaeure mé v'lo un viar grand-père.

Quànd mon frère fut plliechi sis Mess Bourgaise au Four Cabot, comme valet, et que j'étais l'si seul dans la chambre, j'm'avisi d'pendre deaux caûches au pid du llièt, et d'jouaï un "trick" su l''Sandy Claws" qui empllirait les daeux caûches de bouan boucâs, comme il avait ieue amors de faire à la Longue-veille; j'mit un'quéminse de niet bien stoffaïe à mon coteï et un faux visage su l'orillier, mais ch'tait tout en vain, le "Sandy Claws" était pus fin que mé et saqui toute la pêque par l'aire.

Quànd je d'valli pour déjunaï la matinnaïe de Noué. Mes parents mé d'màndirent d'leux mourteï mes persens. Mais j'n'avais rien à mourtaï; et quànd i'découvrirent chu qu'j'avais fait, j'fus bien puni pour aver etaï malhounête, et i m'dounirent que du pain sec et d'auie pour mon denaï auran d'beu rôti et d'la houichepotte à preûne, et d'pis que ch'tait le jour de Noué, j'vous assaeure que ma punition fut grànde. Enfin, ch'tait unn' bouanne leçon pour mé, caer durànt ma vie j'ai etaï pâssâbllement hounête si la tentation n'était poui trop grànde; et après tout, je sis pas le seul qui parfeis fait un faux-pas. La perfection ne s'trouve que dans les Anges au Ciel, sauf le sien qui fut bani pour ne poui s'comportaï comme i faut.

☛

Christmas is coming
by T A Grut

How quickly time passes! It seems to me that it is only a year or two since my brother and I used to hang our stockings at the foot of the bed to be filled by "Sandy Claws" who came down the chimney, and now here I am an old grandfather.

When my brother got a place as valet in the house of Mr. Bourgaise at the Four Cabot, and I was left on my own in the bedroom, I decided to hang two stockings at the foot of the bed, to play a trick on "Sandy Claws" who would fill both stockings with good things, as he liked to do at the "Longue Veille" (December 23rd); I put a well-stuffed night-shirt beside me and a mask on the pillow, but it was all in vain, "Sandy Claws" was craftier than I was and upset my plan.

When I went down to breakfast on Christmas morning, my parents asked me to show them my presents. But I didn't have anything to show; and when they discovered what I had done, I was well punished for having been dishonest, and they gave me dry bread and water for my dinner instead of roast beef and plum pudding, and because it was Christmas Day, I can assure you that my punishment was great. Anyway, it was a good lesson for me, because during my life I have been reasonably honest if temptation has not been too great for me; and after all, I am not the only one who sometimes makes a mistake. Perfection is only found in the Angels in Heaven except for the one who was banished for not behaving as he should.

Chu Noué, j'espère v'ni à la ville atou mes p'tits-effàns pour leux mourtaï les shoppes et les marchis, et p'tête les "pictures," s'i'n'mé coûtent poui trop chiar, caer i'devraient faire unn'réduction sur la quàntitaï, d'pis qy'y en a justement treize à la douzaine, (sept garcons et six filles).

Après chenna, j'leux acat'rai unn'pouquie d'castaïnes rôties, et tandis qu'i s'ront à les mangier, j'm'écapp'rai à la rue d'la Fontaïne pour aver un "p'tit dram." J'espère qu'la Judith n'mé sentira pas, caer al'est teetotaleure, et rouàne si j'prends rien pus fort que l'cidre. Mais, après tout, Noué n'vient qu'un caoup par an, et si je n'saï poui ouqu'est l'autre bord d'la rue, je n's'rai poui l'seul. Et pis, si l'mal vient au pière, les effàns m'condiront à la maison, et pens'ront que ch'est unn'attaque de bile qui m'fait étourdi.

J'vous souhaite un bouan Noué.

Votre ami fidèle
Pierre Langlois
Du Crocq, St. Pierre

This Christmas, I hope to come to Town with my grand-children to show them the shops and the markets, and perhaps the "pictures," if it doesn't cost me too much, because they should make a reduction on the number of them, since there are thirteen of them to the dozen (seven boys and six girls).

After that, I'll buy them a bag of roasted chestnuts, and while they are eating them, I'll escape to Fountain Street to have a "wee dram;" I hope that Judith won't smell it on me because she is teetotal and scolds if I have anything stronger than cider. But after all, Christmas only comes once a year, and if I don't know where the other side of the road is, then I won't be the only one. And then, if the worst comes to the worst, the children will take me home and will think that it's a bilious attack that has made me dizzy.

I wish you a Happy Christmas.

Your faithful friend
Pierre Langlois
Le Crocq, St, Peter's

La raisaon que Dolphus ne maryi pas la Sophie
par Albert Heaume

Pour enne belle p'tite garce, chentai yeune, et le Dolphus l'oimait la Sophie. Nous dit en des temps que l'amour halle pu dur que mille boeux, mais ch'te la veritai en shu cas la. Si l'avait paeux il erait etai la vais tous les saers. I yetait naette achonai.

Ch'te ma chiere par ishin et ma chiere par la, et ils sente l'icotais tant, nous en avait moniere de mal au tcheur. Et savous que en des temps a sassiervait su ses genouaie. Mais enne seraie i furent se pourmenai et la Sophie lie die, "Tu vait Dolphus jenne serait pas que tu moime coume le William oime la Nancy."

"Mais ma chiere quand jerais a sautai par desus chute haeche la, j'le frais pour te."

Ch'te la tchi q'chaose dire pasque ch'te la haeche du chimtiere et a l'avait chins pies d'haut. Y'n savait guerre qui s'nallait l'faire shute seraïe la. Mais quand i chitti la Sophie, il tait aen p'tit pu tard que couteume, et i savai que sen pere sen allait rouanai accore opres tout chenne te q'aen mourse de 25 aens et pour sauvai tchique minutes i decidi d'allai travaer la chimtiere. I faisait biau fin d'leune et i secanchi que l'maite Pierre etait a faire enne fosse et i oui tchi q'un marchier, et justement quand Dolphus passait i denichi sa tete et criyi, "Quai haeure qui l'est?" Dolphus prins la fuite et sauti par dessus la haeche et couorit frans a la maisaon, et quai bas au pid d'lus evoni. Quand sen pere le vit i sachi enne bouctaie d'ioue par su li. I fut pas laongtemp d'vant sevillet.

Pour des jours opres i len saongait diniet. Aen bouan jour i dit a ses gens, "Les sians qui veulent elvai des filles peuvent, mais i peuvent etou les gardaï!"

The reason why Dolphus didn't marry Sophie
by *Albert Heaume*

For a lovely little lass, she was a one, and Dolphus loved Sophie. We say sometimes that love pulls harder than a thousand oxen, but it was the truth in this case. If he had been able he would have seen her every evening. He was completely enslaved.

It was my darling here and my darling there, and they slobbered over each other so much, that we felt nauseous. And do you know that sometimes she sat on his knee. But one evening they went for a walk and Sophie said to him, "You see Dolphus I won't know that you love me as much as William loves Nancy."

"But my darling if I had to jump over that gate over there, I would do it for you."

That was quite something to say because it was the cemetery gate and it was five feet high. He had no idea what he was going to do that evening. But when he left Sophie, it was a little later than usual, and he knew that his father would scold him more because after all he was only a 25 year old lad and to save a few minutes he decided to go through the cemetery. It was bright moon-light and it happened that master Pierre was digging a grave and he heard someone walking by, and just as Dolphus passed by he poked his head out and called, "What time is it?" Dolphus took off and jumped over the gate and ran straight home, and fell down on the door-step in a faint. When his father saw him he threw a bucketful of water over him. It wasn't long before he woke up.

For days afterwards he dreamt about it at night. One fine day he said to his parents, "Those who want to bring up girls may do so, but they can keep them as well!"

Yeune de mes experiences a l'ecole
par Albert Heaume

Malgre que j'en sie pas bien vier (viaille) j'ai enne avis à vous dounnai. Quand vous disai d'chai endrai des jeaunes gens b'sai vos paroles, si vous piais; auterment vous pourraite bien vite nous mette dans d'yeau caude. N'en v'chain enne instance: l'aute jour à l'ecole la maitresse dis, "Aucheux qui peuve répaondre ma question errons six merques. Chic est ain miracre?"

J'avais oui men paire dire à ma maire l'aute sair et alhaure j'mis ma main a haux, et la maitresse dis, "Eh bien (ten nom) chic est la répaunce?" et j'lis, "Si vous n'aitte pas marrais au jeaune ministre d'vans jamais 3 mais d'ichin, et bian chen s'ra la ain miracre."

Savous qu'ante pas contente, et ame dis, "P'tit/e impudent/e." mais j'lis dis, "Chez la veritai parce que s'tai mon paire qu'il disait a ma maire l'aute sair, et s'ait qu'ma maire dis, "J'mettais aperchue qu'a n'a quaid l'y sautai dans les pautes."★

Eh bien, ame dounni mes 6 merques. Et quain j'er vains a la maison, j'le dis a ma maire et am'pichi accourre enne chac et m'envyit au yait. A's trouvi a la chamber justement quand j'soais dans l'yait et am dis, "Ya chenna, j'vé que t'as tes 6 merques terjous, v'la qu'est tout bian, mais gache à pan n'ya pas rian en rire."

★ Guernsey idiom

One of my experiences at school
by Albert Heaume

Although I am not very old, I have some advice to give you. When you say something in front of young people, consider your words if you please; otherwise you could land us in hot water. Here is an instance: the other day at school, the teacher said, "Anyone who can answer my question will receive 6 marks. What is a miracle?"

I had heard my father say it to my mother the other evening and at once I put my hand up, and the teacher said, "Well (name) what is the answer?" and I said to her, "If you are not married to the young minister before 3 months from now, well it will be a miracle."

Do you know she wasn't pleased and said to me, "Impudent child," but I said to her, "It's the truth because it was my father who was telling my mother the other evening, and my mother said, "I had noticed that she was about to jump into his pockets. (she was throwing herself at him)."

Well, she gave me my 6 marks. When I came home, I told my mother and she gave me a smack and sent me to bed. She came into the bedroom just as I was jumping into bed and said, "There's one thing, I see that you got your 6 marks anyway, that's all very well, but it's nothing to laugh about."

19

Les Omelettes
par Doris O Heaume

Ma Graenmère nou avé terjous contai, que quend a s'mari il avez etta en France sé pourmenai et qui l'avé visitai Le Mont St Michel et la avez ieux des superbe omelettes faite par la exquisite cuisinière Mde Poullain q'été couneuse partou l'monde pour ces omelette. Comme disé Graenmère, "chuque q'il tes bouanne dequié coume nou n'avé joimais goutai d'van." Et pie s'fai t'alle, tout orguieuse, "Mde Poullain vint nou paslai, et quend a vi combian interessie q'j'étais a dounni la r'cette."

Mais donc, joimais nou la veuse, ni goutai. Omelette different a chuque Mam faisé, biauc Graenmère d'muré dauve non et bian souvent faisé la cook'rie.

Alice ma soeur travalié sur la ferme, nou avé enne gauine de vacs, et pie mé j'agais a Mam a faire le bure et les cialbots, et abeurva les viaux.

Aen bouan jour quaend pape et mam avez acata le courti Moullin, y vint enne letter l'Avocat pour les averti se trouva en cour, le venderdi, pour passaie contra, la pensai m'vint, sré sans doute Graenmère qui preparai l'dainai, et venderdi y'avé pas grand frico, di a Alice, "vla note chanse, chette faie, fau donc li d'manda d'nou faire des omelettes a la maniere du Mont St Michel. A sen est terjours ventaie, nou verra donc si rellement a la la r'cette."

Alice été d'idee et nou decidi arrettai pour le ser quaend a sré a ouvra sen corset d'oeuvre, et taille afaire. A l'été d'bouan humeur, si fiere que pape avé acata l'courti du Maitre Thoumas.

(pointing hand symbol)

Omelettes
by Doris O Heaume

My Grandmother had always told us that when she was married they had gone to France on holiday and that they had visited Mont St Michel and they had had some superb omelettes made by the exquisite cook Madame Poullain who was known all over the world for her omelettes. As Grandmother said, "Weren't they good, something which we had never had before." And then she said, very proudly, "Madame Poullain came to talk to us, and when she saw how interested I was, she gave me the recipe."

Well now, we have never seen it, or tasted an omelette different from that which Mother made, even though Grandmother lived with us and very often did the cooking.

Alice my sister worked on the farm, we had a large number of cows, and I helped mother to make the butter and the curds, and to give water to the calves.

One fine day when Father and Mother had bought the Moullin field, a letter came from the Advocate to advise them to be in court on Friday, to pass contracts, and the thought came to me, no doubt it will be grandmother who will prepare the dinner, and that on Fridays there wasn't a great feast, so I said to Alice, "Now is our chance, this time, let's ask her to make us some omelettes in the manner of Mont St Michel. She has always boasted about them, now let's see if she really has the recipe."

Alice agreed and we decided to wait for the evening when she would be knitting her guernsey, and such things. She was in a good mood, so pleased that Father had bought the field from Mr. Thomas.

J'li d'mandi après chic minute, si a sen aller faire le dainai venderdi, et a me gardi pardessu ses lunette, "Oui, sans doute," a repondi, "et pourchi tu veur save?" cam'di.

"Alice et mé, nou oimerais a vou vest faire des omelette, coume vou avaiz ieux en France. Vou avai sans doute acore la r'cette a chic bord."

A fu ravi la d'mande q'nou fi, mais promisi oui, ca nou en fré pour daina. Tous été leva boaun partemps le venderdi matin. Pape et Mam parti pour la ville bouane eure. Alice et mé fini du trava par dix eure, en esperant aigier a Graenmère q'été deja brachi au coute bian enbarasaie a ramassai tou chuque qui fallait, enne bouan douzaine d'oeus, enne grande mogie d'lait, dla fieur et dans aen papier dla brune poudre, et du limon. Je mis pour aiger, mais ch'est qu'a n'té pas fiere. "Veyou fille d'aoute bord dla table, j'né pas besoin d'aige," et au bord d'la grande baule a s'mie a craquier l'oeu iun après l'aute, et ajouta les aute afaire. Biautot a déhalli enne p'tit bouteille de sa pote, et versi dans la baule chichose q'avé hardi bouan sent, et pie a s'mi a batte sans arrettai, pour aen cinq minutes. En été rouge dans l'visage.

La peille q'été su l'stove q'menchi a fuma et biautot a versi enne coupas du melange dans la peille. Chuque menvais vou dire y'avé aen bouan sent, ch't'e enne fishu gros omelette tou different a chuque mam faisé, tou eux couc, v'la un tappe al'us, chiqun, di a graenmère et au meme temps enne voix cri, "Est tou la Madame?"

I asked, after a few minutes, if she was going to make the dinner on Friday, and she looked at me over her glasses, "Yes, no doubt," she replied, "and why do you want to know?" she said to me.

"Alice and I, we'd like you to see you make some omelettes like you had in France. No doubt you have still got the recipe somewhere."

She was surprised at the request we made, but promised that yes, she would make us some for our dinner. Everyone was up very early on Friday morning. Father and Mother left for Town in good time. Alice and I finished work by ten o'clock, hoping to help Grandmother who had already rolled up her sleeves to the elbow and was busy collecting all that was needed, a good dozen eggs, a large jug of milk, some flour and in a paper some brown powder, and some lemon. I began to help, but she wasn't pleased. "Look here girls, on the other side of the table. I don't need any help," and she began to the crack eggs one after the other on the edge of the large bowl, and added them to the other things. Soon she took a little bottle out of her pocket, and poured something which had a good smell into the bowl, and then she began to beat it for a good five minutes. She became all red in the face.

The frying pan which was on the stove began to smoke and soon she poured a cupful of the mixture in to the pan. Well I can tell you that there was a lovely smell, it was a great big omelette, very different from those Mother made. Suddenly, there was a knock at the door, I said to Grandmother that there was someone there, and at the same time a voice called "Are you there madam?"

Chuque a té marie la poure veille, quaend a vi l'ministre entrai. Il avé terjous la maniere d'allai vest duran la s'moine si chiqun la famille n'été pas a leglise dimanche. Mai donc bian gervaie grenmare li di s'assie et y mi a pie dla table dans la p'tit chaire. Et mis a d'visa a grenmère atour la pourmenai pour les veille gens, et si a li viandre. Ch'té pour avé thé a l'Ancresse le jeudi en v'nant, pour sorti leglise a daeux eure et quar, les tiquet été 2/6. Graenmère pouvé pas decidai, a trouve qui faise fré dans la bus ouvert.

Nou c'menchi a senti un sent brula et cri si dur q'et fi Graenmère sauta. Ses pensai bian yiau l'omelette, a l'attrape la peille et immediatement sauti l'omelette jusque au celin. Jen tena n'aloin quaend la vi d'valla. Savé vraiement bian ca retourne pas dans la peille. Nai ch'te dans la grande baule ca sen fu et justement equiavini minitre et non tou. Et pour agva l'afaire Graenmère tappe la baule dauve la peille, qui la culbuti et a fu buchi. Chuque yiau avé du ménage par la cuisiane. Le ministre été bu a seloque. Poure Graenmère, il est vrai a fu baquie. Après avé tourchi nos hardes Alice et mé nou lavi la cuisiane et Pape et Mam entée dla ville et debu dans lus.

"Qui malportai qui ces arriva?" Mam regardi sa belle baule q'été bian buchi mis a pieura. Graenmère pouvez pas d'visa. A fu l'sise au dire histoire, et au jour enyier nou na pas acore goutai ché fameuse omelette du Mont St Michel.

Well, she was furious, the poor old lady, when she saw the minister come in. He always had the habit of going to see during the week why someone in the family wasn't in church on Sunday. Well, very annoyed, Grandmother told him to sit down and he went to the end of the table and sat in the little chair. He began to speak to Grandmother about the old peoples' outing, and if she would go. They would have tea at L'Ancresse next Thursday, leaving the church at quarter past two, the tickets cost 2/6. Grandmother couldn't decide, she thought that it was cold in the open bus.

We began to smell burning and I called out so loudly that it made Grandmother jump. Her thoughts very far from the omelette, she grasped the frying pan and immediately threw the omelette up to the ceiling. I held my breath when I saw it come down. I knew very well that it would not return to the frying pan. No, it was in the large bowl that it went and splashed the minister and all of us. And to make matters worse, Grandmother knocked the bowl with the frying pan, which upset it and it was smashed. Well, there was a to-do in the kitchen. The minister was standing up using bad language. Poor Grandmother, it's true that she was taken aback. After having wiped our clothes, Alice and I, we washed the kitchen, and Father and Mother came back from Town and were standing in the doorway.

"What on earth has been happening?" Mother looked at her lovely bowl which was all smashed and began to cry. Grandmother was speechless. She was left to tell the story, and up to now we haven't yet tasted this famous omelette from Mont St Michel.

Les neufs genouais de ma faumme
par Barry Hockey

Quand j'vins du travais, je vis ma faumme à maette daeux sacs déhors, près du dustbin. Quand a vint en d'dans, a dit, "Caw chapin, mes genouais, faont-i ma!"

J'y dis, "J'sis pas ravi. J't'ai dit d'vant, tu devrais prend riocque aen sac par caoup." Ch'n'est pas bian que les faummes aont à travaillier si dur, veis-tu!

Aen p'tit-au- caoup, les genouais empierirent et a fut au docteur. All'aeut des X-rays, et des tests pour son sang, et i li dit que le genouais d'gaouche devrait ête rempiechi. Mais all'tait genaie!

Quand a l'dit à sen p'tit-éfànt, i li dit ," Gran'mère, s'en vaont-i copaïr le genouai et l'houlaïr sous la tablle?"

Eh bian, chena la gênit passequ'a savait que ch'tait enne terrible operatiaon e ta n'voulait pas ouir t'ché d'mesme.

Eh bian, all'aeut l'operatiaon et all'amendit raide bian.

Auprès quasi quatre meis, all'avait amendaï et pas d'aute de ma, mais all'avait a s'méfiaïr passeque le genouai gaouche allait pus vit que le sian dêtre, et all'erait paeux allaïr en raond comme enne piroue.

Quasi huit meis auprès, a fut dit que le genouai dêtre devrait ête rempiechi ossi vite qué possible.

J'i dis, "D'mande au docteur si j'peux aver l'ôs pour faire enne "bean-jar."

Quand a d'visit au docteur enn'haeure auprès l'operatiaon, all'i dit, "Du merci que j'sie pas enne vaque au cas j'érais acore daeux genouais à faire!"

Ma faumme a enne belle pare de neufs genuoais aucht'haeure. Mais i faut qu'a s'méfie quand a danse "Knees up, Mother Brown" passequ'i vaont pus vite que le reste d'ielle!

20

My wife's new knees
by Barry Hockey

When I came home from work, I saw my wife putting two sacks outside for the dustbin. When she came inside, she said, "Good gracious, my knees are hurting."

I said to her " I'm not surprised. I've told you before that you should take one sack at a time." It's not right that women have to work so hard, you see!

Gradually, her knees got worse and she went to the doctor. She had some X-rays and some blood tests and he told her that her left knee should be replaced. Wasn't she frightened!

When she told her grand-child, he said to her, "Grandma, are they going to cut off the knee and throw it under the table?"

Well, that frightened her because she knew that it was a terrible operation and she didn't want to hear things like that.

Well, she had the operation and she improved very well.

After nearly four months, she had improved and had no more pain, but she had to be careful because the left knee went faster than the right one and she would have been able to go round like a spinning top.

Almost eight months later she was told that the right knee had to be replaced as soon as possible.

I told her, "Ask the doctor if I can have the bone to make a bean-jar."

When she spoke to the doctor after the operation, she said to him," Thank goodness that I'm not a cow or else I would have two more knees to-do!"

My wife has a lovely pair of knees now. But she has to be careful when she dances "Knees up, Mother Brown" because they go faster than the rest of her!

L'Haomme et le Perrotchet
par Barry Hockey

Enn haomme fut d'mandaï à souognier aen perrotchet pour tchicun qui s'n allait pour aen holiday. Le perrotchet d'visait bian, mais ch'tait pas tout – il jurait comme aen "rebel de Rocquoine."

Pour aver d'la paix, il mit le perrotchet dans énn aoute endret, mais il criait acore pus dur et baillait des bougaons.

Aen jour, le perrotchet le guervit tant dauve son mauvais d'vis, qu'il le mit dans le cabinet sous les dégrais, dans le nar.

"Là," s'fit-il, "chena t'apprendra. Tu sortiras quand t'eras apprins à te taire (restaïr trantchille)."

Le perrotchet criait et jurait à tue tête. Il commenchit à grataïr l'hu dauve ses grifffes et il erachait de grands morciaux dauve son bec, qui fait l'haomme fut oblligi de le lessier sortir.

Après tchiques jours l'affaire n'avait pas changi et l'haomme décidit qu'il était temps tchique chaose de pus dur, parce qu'il s'en allait aver d'la visite. Il aeut en bouanne idée. Il mettrait le perrotchet dans le "freezer".

Le mouisaon n'était pas fiar et il criait et hurlait et jurait pour tchique temps-pis tout fut trantchille!

Après dix minutes l'haomme fut gênaï et il voulait saver chu qu'était arrivaï au perrotchet. Il fut à le "freezer", ouvrisit l'hu et r'gardit d'dans Le perrotchet y était assis, tout trantchille. L'haomme y mit sa moin, halit le perrotchet et le remit dans sa cage. Le mouisaon ne dit pas erion, mais il regardit le "freezer" tristement.

Après quasi enne haeure l'haomme a oui le perrotchet qui disait à li même, "Mondou, je sais pas chu que chute paure dinde là-d'dans erait pai faire!"

21

The man and the parrot
by Barry Hockey

A man was asked to look after a parrot for someone who was going on holiday. The parrot talked well, but that was not all – it swore like a "Rocquaine Rebel."

To have some peace, he put the parrot in another room, but it shouted even louder and screamed out bad words.

One day the parrot annoyed him so much with its bad language, that he put it in the cupboard under the stairs, in the dark.

"There," he said, "that will teach you. You'll come out when you learn to be quiet."

The parrot screamed and swore at the top of its voice. It began to scratch at the door with its claws and chewed big chunks with its beak, so the man had to let it out.

After a few days, things hadn't changed and the man decided that it was time for more drastic action because he was going to have some visitors. He had a good idea. He would put the parrot in the freezer.

The bird was not pleased and it screamed, shouted and swore for a long time and then it was quiet!

After ten minutes, the man got worried and he wanted to know what had happened to the parrot. He went to the freezer and opened the door and looked in. The parrot was sitting there, very quietly. The man put in his hand, took out the parrot and put it back in its cage. The bird said nothing, but looked sadly at the freezer.

After almost an hour, the man heard the parrot say to itself, "My God, I can't think what that poor turkey in there could have done!"

Ma Gran'mère et mon Gran'père
(par les iaers d'en enfant)
par Barry Hockey

Ma Gran'mère et mon Gran'père, il saont les millias dans tout l' maonde.

Y a pas des hardes que ma Gran'mère peut pas ouvraïr ou faire, et y a pas autcheun qui peut coutcher comme ielle.

Mon Gran'père peut ramendaïr autcheun chaose et sait tout chaose. Si nous l'i d'mande i peut terjous répaondre, mais, s'ra pas terjous la veritaï, pasque i nous caont terjous des lures.

J'sis fiar que j'vivais pas dans les temps quand il'taient jonne, pas qu'ils'taient très stricte, et il avaient à mangier des sprouts et d'la caboche. Boudiax!

Il'taient enn amas mauvais, mais j'sis pas ravi qu'il'taient terjous en broue dauve laeux père et les maîtraesses.

Les qu'vaeux de ma Gran'mère aont changi, quand al'tait jonne il'taient naer, mais auchteure i saont bllu.

Quand a dit qu'a s'en va courre, ch'est pas en avant qu'a va, ch'est pus-s-a caoup en haout et en bas.

Mon Gran'père est trop haout pour ses qu'vaeux, sa rille est si grande qué il demêle ses qu'vaeux dauve son flonet.

Il a des neuves dents et il est terjous à les hallaïr pour mourtaïr ès gens dans l'endret son biau souris.

Mon Gran'père dit qu'il est viaer, i n'est pas pasque son visage n'est pas ratchi.

Ma Gran'mere dit que tout chuque al'a est grand, mais, ch'est pas vrai, pasque ses pentoreilles saont enn amas p'tites.

Ah! Mais que j'les oime, ma Gran'mère et mon Gran'père. Ils saont les millias dans tout l'maonde!

My Grandma and my Grandpa (through the eyes of a child)
by Barry Hockey

My Grandma and my Grandpa are the best people in all the world.

There aren't any clothes that my Grandma can't knit or make, and nobody else can cook like her.

My Grandpa can mend anything and knows everything there is to know. He is never stuck for an answer, but it may not all be true because he is always pulling my leg.

I'm glad that I didn't live in the days when they were young because it was too strict and they had to eat brussels-sprouts and cabbage. Boudiax! (Ugh!)

They were really naughty and it was no wonder that they got into trouble with their parents and teachers.

Grandma's hair has changed, when she was young it was black, now it is blue.

When she says she is running, she doesn't go forward much, rather she goes up and down.

Grandpa is getting too tall for his hair. His parting is so wide that he combs his hair with a face flannel.

He's got new teeth which he keeps taking out to show the other people in the room his wonderful smile.

Grandpa says he is old, but he isn't because his face doesn't look worn out.

Grandma says everything she has is big, but that isn't true because her earrings are small!

I really love them. They are simply the best. My Grandma and my Grandpa.

Le téléphone
par Joe du Moullin (J Hervé)

Men frère avais aën ami qui étais bian malade. Son näom étais Henri. I vensus de mortri. Tom, le frère d'Henri, dit qui fallais allaï faire des arrangements pour l'entèrrement, vère, y fut vèe le fossaëux.

Aprais avait d'visaïr pour aën p'tit d'temps, le fossaëux li d'mandi sil pouvait affordaïr pour payer la fosse, suffaïe est si chier ogniet.

Tom li dit que perchoin pour il y arais li baïller aën côd'môin à fair la fosse. Mais quand il arrivit au chaëmtière, la pierre étais défonsaïe.

"Et bien bon," s'fi Tom,"il faudra la mette draëtte d'moin. En attendand, il faudra l'amarraïr d'âuve aen wire."

I l'amarrïre à aën arbre qui étais tout près d'la fosse. Enfin deux haömmes passire durent la niet. Il vire le wire en r'viant du club.

S'fi iun des deux, "Cor, ils aönt même mit le téléphone!"

The telephone
by Joe du Moullin (J Hervé)

My brother had a friend who was very ill. His name was Henry. He had just died. Tom, Henry's brother, said that they had to go and make arrangements for the funeral, so he went to see the gravedigger.

After having talked for a little while, the gravedigger asked him if he could afford to pay for the grave, because snuffing it is so expensive nowadays.

Tom told him that the next day, he would go and give him a hand to dig the grave. But when he arrived at the cemetery, the stone had collapsed.

"Well then," said Tom, "we'll have to put it straight tomorrow. For the time being we'll have to tie it up with wire."

He tied it to a tree which was near the grave. However, two men passed by during the night. They saw the wire when returning from the club.

Said one of the two, "Cor, they've even put in the 'phone!"

Quand la gière c'menchier
par *Joe du Moullin (J Hervé)*

Men fu aen travas dans la ferme. J'avais seize vacque, deux guédos d'auve des p'tits guédos; des poules, des pirattes, deux lapins et aen mauvais tchen. I n'oimaïr pas les Allemands.

Men prumier job à faire état à pointuraïr aen grinaöuse. Aprés avais traire les vacques, fallait allaïr à la derie.

Aen jour, le maître me d'mandaïr d'allaïr sie aen faume d'auve aen bouteille de lait, et a m'dounera äen douzaine d'oeus.

La faire allair bien, mais quand j'vis en fache de la shoppe de Valpy, j'avais amarrair le tchen d'auve äen corde à men bike.

Quand i vi le cat, le tchen s'arouti souvent le cat et je m'en fut par dessus les pouognis; mais oeus et le lait tout à travers la rue et men bike dans le fossaï.

J'paraisais ma fé bien, et les soudarts Allemand rirer coume des perdus. Quand j'arrivair à la ferme, iaeu du camas; et le maitre me douni l'sac.

I ya enamas que j'pourais vous r'caontaïr atouor l'Occupatiaon!

24

When the war began
by Joe du Moullin (J Hervé)

I went to work on the farm. I had sixteen cows, two pigs with some little pigs; some hens, some ducks, two rabbits and a wicked dog. He didn't like the Germans.

My first job was to paint a greenhouse. After having milked the cows, I had to go to the dairy.

One day, the master asked me to go to a woman's house with a bottle of milk and she would give me a dozen eggs.

Everything was going well, but when I arrived in front of Valpy's shop, I tied the dog to my bike with a rope.

When he saw the cat, the dog started off after the cat and I went over the handlebars; the eggs and the milk were all across the road and my bike in the hedge.

My word, I looked well, and the German soldiers were laughing their heads off. When I arrived at the farm, there was trouble and the master gave me the sack.

There are a lot of things I could tell you about the Occupation!

Un jour a Candie
par *Joe du Moullin (J Hervé)*

Un Jour, Jim décidi d'allaïr fair un tour pour la ville. S'fait t'il "J'prin en taxi qui passè pa si mé, et j'dite au chauffeur, 'Tu peu mett bas auprès l'Arsenal d'la ville'."

"Et bien oui," s'fait il. J'marchs au le gardin dans Candie. Dévan d'commenchier mas tour, j'mé décidit d'avë un coupaïe d'thée, et un morcé d'gache et un gallette à beurre. Il' yon avait pas, qui fait j'demandi un dora d'beurre et d'gla.

J'étais assi dehors, dans le rondage q'il'y a auprés du restaurant. Un moussieu si trouvi étout; le paure maufé, il avais un gambe de bois. I'mé di q'en moto avais passaie sur sa gambe, et l'avait rompu. J'en avait bein de regret. J'li demandi s'il oimait Candie, et i di q'oui.

Biento il s'trouvi enemas de gens, qui fait j'li dit,"Vous m'excusera, j'menvais an p'tit pus y'en,"et j'li souhaites le bon jour.

J'menfus après dans le fond du gardin vais les belles fieurs qui y' avais la – des tulips, et d'la violette et des minionettes – c'est magnifique. Le printempts, à mon avis, c'est la plus belle de l'anné. Un petit après j'fus vais les piessons. Il'yavais pas moyon d'les contais, y'en avais bientrops.

Auprès la brecq de bas, envier la statue de Victor Hugo, il y avait un banc. J'pensi, "Bon, il faudra sassiet dessus. Quand nous pense a shu grand homme là, venu d' la France pour demeurraï ichen."

A day at Candie
by Joe du Moullin (J Hervé)

One day, Jim decided to go on a visit to Town. He said, "I took a taxi which passed my house, and I said to the driver, 'You can put me down by the Arsenal in Town'."

"Alright," he said. I walked in the garden at Candie. Before beginning my tour, I decided to have a cup of tea, a piece of gâche and a Guernsey biscuit. They didn't have any, so I asked for a sandwich of butter and jam.

I was sitting outside on the round terrace near the restaurant. A gentleman came there as well; the poor wretch, he had a wooden leg. He told me that a car had gone over his leg and it had been broken. I was really sorry for him. I asked him if he liked Candie and he said, "Yes."

Soon a lot of people came, so I said to him, "You will excuse me, I am going a little further on," and I bade him good-day.

Afterwards I went to the bottom of the garden to see the beautiful flowers there – tulips, violets and mignonette – it's magnificent. Spring, in my opinion, is the most beautiful season. A little later I went to see the fish. There was no way to count them, there were too many of them.

Near the lower gate, towards the statue of Victor Hugo, there is a bench. I thought, "Good, I must sit on it. When we think that great man came from France to live here."

J'étais endormis sur le banc quand une femme mé chachit. Mais chette femme m'éffriei, elle avait un si grand chapé et des lunetts. A s'assievi auprès d'mé. A mé demandi si j'mé souvenet de 1912. "Oui," j'li dit, "à la ville quand mon père mavais mis sur ses épaules pour mé à vèe la fiotte Française quit etait sur la rade."

Saint Julien était toute allumaïe chette serra la, des grand lanterne et des petits partout. A m'dit qe ch'tait les soudart Anglais qui mit la statue à sa pièce. Les soudarts était stationni au Chaté Cornet. a petit après, la femme s'en fut et mé lessi là tout seul.

J'm'en fut examiner la statue; mais quand nous vais la beauti. Victor Hugo a son chapé dans la main; sa capette vo au vent, et pis son baton en biue rocque étout. Eun de ce bouane jour jirais vais sa maison à Hauteville.

L'écriture sur la statue peu vous faire pensi à chu qui dit, "Au rocher d'hospitalité, de liberté. A ce coin de vieille terre Normande òu vit le noble petit people de la mer. L'île de Guernesey, sévère et douce."

D'ichen fit mon ch'min envier la breck de haut. Devant de sorti, fut vais la statue de Sa Maiesté, la Royne Victoria. J'gards à ma montre-comme le temps s'passe, quand nous es à visitie.

Enfin, j'passs par le gren hotel qui s'trouve sur le coin, "Richmond," j'cré qui s'appel.

J'mé trouvi en haute des Côtils, dans le rondage, et j'pensis, "Quail belle veu, d'auve les îles et les petits bateaux au poission, et d'autre à faire des tours."

Dichin j'me fut pour ma bus après avais passaï une bouanne harleva.

I was asleep on the bench when a woman shook me. How that woman scared me, she had such a big hat and glasses. She sat down next to me. She asked me if I remembered 1912. "Yes," I said to her, "in Town when my father put me on his shoulders so that I could see the French fleet which was in the roads." (Anchorage)

St. Julian's was all lit up that evening; there were big and small lanterns everywhere. She told me that it was the English soldiers who had put the statue in its place. The soldiers were stationed at Castle Cornet. A little later, the woman went off and left me on my own.

I went to examine the statue; when we see the beauty! Victor Hugo has his hat in his hand; his cape is flying in the wind and then his stick is in blue granite as well. One of these days, I will go and see his house at Hauteville.

The writing on the statue makes you think of what he said, "To the rock of hospitality, of liberty. To this corner of this ancient Norman land where lives the noble little people of the sea. The island of Guernsey, severe yet sweet."

From here, I made my way towards the upper gate. Before going out, I went to see the statue of Her Majesty, Queen Victoria. I looked at my watch-how time passes when you are on a visit.

At last I passed by the big hotel on the corner, "Richmond" I think it's called.

I found myself at the top of the Cotils, on the terrace, and I thought, "What a lovely view, with the islands and the little fishing boats, and others on trips."

From here, I went for my bus having spent a good afternoon.

Les chàngements du drôin sièclle
par Renée Jehan

Ichin d'vànt, tous marchaient à pid, ou allaient à ch'va. Les gens d'travas allaient éiouque le travas était su les daëux pids. Et pis, le motor car arrivit. J'm'en r'meis qué, quand nous oyer aen motor hootaï en faisànt le raond, nous arroutait à la braëque pour le veis passaïr. Auchtaëure, l'île en bouit.

A l'arrivànt du motor, les rues qu'menchirent à ête tarraies. Prumièrement, les grandes rues pour les bus, et pis les p'tites rues. Dans les prumières bus, nous s'assièait tout l'tour, et les degräis en derrière. Les droîns éfants qui v'naient, s'assièvaient su les degräis. Chena n's'r'ait pas allouaï auchtaëure. Y'avait les bus "Lorina," les "Greys" et les "Guernsey Motors" pour le vouest; les "Bluebird, Paragon et Guensey Railway" pour le nord.

Es écoles d'la càmpoigne, tous parlaient le guernésiais, et si tchiques éfants arrivaient, il'appernaient vite. D's éfants apprennent vite parmi leurs sorte.

Ma mémouaïre va au prumier telephone. Ch'tait aen boxe dauve enne chignolle au cotaï qu'i fallait tournaïr pour ête connectaï à l'exchange, et i fallait dire le numéro que nous voulait pour ête connectaï. Que nous pouvait d'visaïr à tchiqu'un qu'était ailleurs était aen miracle.

Les planes étou. Quand ieune passait l'île haout dans le ciel, nous courait vite dehors pour la veis. Ch'tit rémarkablle.

☛

Changes of the last century
by Renée Jehan

Formerly, we travelled on foot or on a horse. Workers went to wherever the work was on their two feet. Then the motorcar arrived. I remember that when we heard a car hooting whilst turning the corner, we went to the gate to see it pass. Now the island is full of them.

After the arrival of the car, the roads began to be covered with tarmac. First the wide roads for the bus, and then the small roads. In the first bus as we sat all around them, with the steps at the back. The last children who came sat on the steps. That would not be allowed now. There were the buses from "Lorina", the "Greys" and the "Guernsey Motors" for the west, the "Bluebird", "Paragon" and "Guernsey Railway" for the north.

At the country schools, we spoke Guernsey-French, and if any children arrived, they learned it quickly. Children learn quickly among their peers.

My memory goes to the first telephone. It was a box with a handle at the side which we had to turn to be connected to the exchange, and we had to say the number that we wanted to be connected. That we could speak to someone who was elsewhere was a miracle.

The planes as well. When one passed over the island, high in the sky, we ran outside quickly to see it. It was remarkable!

I fut décidaï pour le progrès de l'île qu'i fallait enn'aérodrome. Il'tait tchestiaon si s'rait à la Villiaze ou à l'Erée. Par enne voie dauve bian d'la dispute, i décidirent à la Villiaze. Enne maisaon, "Milestone House," fut démolie, et l'oeuvre pour faire enn'airport qu'menchit. Il'tait bian fini quand les Allemands arrivirent. Le temps des Allemands était aen temps d'écarsitaï pour toutes chaoses, et nous rjouit de leur depart oprès chinque ans. Dépis chena, l'airport a augmentaï et i va auchtaeure de St. Andri à Pllaisànce.

Aen grand changement était l'arrivaïe du "wireless." Que nous pouvait ouïr les nouvelles du jour instàntment de partout l'maonde était enn'aoüte miraclle. Chena fut suivi par la télévisiaon en naer et biànc, et pus tard, en couleur. Nous a vaie, étou, enn'haomme à marchier su la leune! Et pis, les computers que nous vieillards n'y counnissent vaer ni gris!

Le progrès marche tout l'temps, et n'y a qu'i sache quaï changements les jonnes gens véraont dans leurs temps.

It was decided for the progress of the island that we needed an aerodrome. It was a question of if it would be at La Villiaze or at L'Erée. By one vote, with a lot of dispute, they decided on La Villaize. A house called "Milestone House" was demolished, and the work to build an airport began. It was quite finished when the Germans arrived. The time of the Germans was a time of scarcity for everything and we rejoiced at their departure after five years. Since then, the airport has grown and now goes from St. Andrews to Plaisance.

A great change was the arrival of the wireless. That we could hear the news of the day instantly from everywhere in the world was another miracle. That was followed by the television in black and white, and later, in colour. We have also seen a man walking on the moon! And then, the computers, about which we "oldies" don't understand a single thing!

Progress marches on all the time, and who knows what changes the young people will see during their lifetime.

27

Aen Tour en Europe
par Robert Langlois

Mon père Dudley, était dans l'armaïe duràunt la drôine djère. En dix-neuf chents tchéràunte-quate i débartchit à Graye-sur-Mer en Normandie tchiques jours oprès D-Day. Par dégraïs i passit à travaers la Fràunce, la Belgique, la Hollàunde et finalement aussi llian qué Hanover en Allemogne. I n'fut pas démobilisaï d'vàunt l'étai dé tchéràunte-saept.

Dad faisait bian d's amis partout éiouque son dévouaer lé print, partitchullièrement en Fràunce et en Belgique parce qu'i parlait lé "bouan fràunçais" enne amas bian. Au c'menchement d'tchéràunte-huit, mouoins d'enne onnaïe oprès avé tchittaï l'armaïe, i décidit qu'i voudrait r'tournaïr pour veies comme tchi qu'ches bouans gens, qu'avaient tàunt souffert, faisaient. Ma mère, Freda, était d'accord, qui fait, le meis d'août nous v'là dauve not p'tit Vauxhall à bord du *Brittany* en route pour Saint Malo. Pour mon p'tit frère Jean, qu'avait riocque six ans, et pour mé, tres ans pus viaer, ch'tait notte prumière visite en Europe.

Partout en Normandie i'y avait acore des saegnes d'la djère. Des 'tank' et des ouadgins tous rouis abàundounnaïs dans les fossaïs, énn amas d'tranchies et d''bunkers', tout plloins d'bâtiments rouinnaïs, d's arbres sàuns caomptaïr endoummagis par la till'rie. Dé l'aoute cotaï i'y avait les spéctaclles traditionnelles comme des Calvaires, des viaers châtés, des fermes et des gràunges dauve des faits en glli, des biaux gardins à poummiers pour faire le cidre et des laongs tchériots tâssaïs d'bllaï, tout qui faisait enne magnifique picture.

A Tour in Europe
by Robert Langlois

My father, Dudley, was in the army during the last war. In nineteen forty-four he landed at Graye-sur-Mère in Normandy a few days after D-Day. Gradually he moved up through France, Belgium, Holland and finally as far as Hanover in Germany. He was not demobilised until the summer of forty-seven.

Dad made many friends wherever his duty took him, particularly in France and Belgium because he spoke "good French" very well. At the beginning of forty-eight, less than a year after leaving the army, he decided that he would like to go back to see how those good people who had suffered so much, were getting along. My mother, Freda, was in agreement, so in the month of August, there we were with our little Vauxhall on board the *Brittany* heading for Saint Malo. For my little brother, John, who was only six years old, and for me, three years older, it was our first visit to Europe.

Everywhere in Normandy there were still signs of the war. Tanks and lorries all rusty abandoned in the hedges, many trenches and bunkers, and lots of ruined buildings, countless trees damaged by the shellfire. On the other hand there were traditional sights like Calvaires, old chateaux, farms and barns with thatched roofs, beautiful cider orchards and long carts piled high with corn, which all made a marvellous picture.

Chaque gniet nous restit dauve enne fomille qué Dad counnissait, et i'y avait aen grànd festin à notte hounneur. Le cri ch'tait "Ah, le libérateur est revenu!" Ch'tait daonc enne expérience, et nous vit bian la vie d'la càmpogne d'la Frànce, qu'était acore pus simplle en chu temps-là. Les légeumes en route pour lé marchi dans des chivières, les haommes à copaïr l'herbe dauve lé faoux, des paisaons dauve des sabots d'bouais et graïs tout en naer, et naturellement la p'tite maisaon déhors. Vous savaïz comme tchi directe les Français peuvent ête en des temps. Et bian, aen caoup Dad était assis tràntchillement sus "l'traone", et v'là la faumme du fermier qui marche en d'dans sàns cérémonie et li daonne un mouchet d'papier, en disànt qu'alle avait raombillai d'lé rempiéchier l'matin.

Mesme auch't'haeure, à peu près sésànte ans pus tard, nous est acore amis dauve tchiqu'uns d'ches bouans gens-là, la faumme étout qui lâtchit tcheies sa caunne à lait en étaonn'ment quand Dudley li d'màndit en français du bord d'la rue pour d's oeus pour ses camarades. A criyit, "Mon Dieu, un soldat anglais qui parle le français!"

J'pourrais vous r'caontaïr bian pus atour les chaoses excitàntes qu'nous vit en Belgique et en Hollande, mais n'i'y'a pas l'temps, malheuraessement. Durànt l'tchin'jours nous restit dans riocque daeux hôtaels. Biau qu'j'étais si jônne, lé merveillaeux bian-v'nu et la baontaïe qu'nous r'chut resteraont dans ma mémouaire à jomais. "L'Entente Cordiale" était certôinement vivànte en chu temps là!

Each night we stayed with a family which dad knew, and there was a great feast in our honour. The cry went up, "Ah, the liberator has returned!" It was indeed an experience, and we really saw French country life, which was still simpler at that time. Vegetables being taken to market in wheelbarrows, men cutting the grass with scythes, peasants in wooden clogs dressed all in black, and of course outside privies. You know how down-to-earth the French can sometimes be. Well, on one occasion Dad was sitting peacefully on the "throne", when, without ceremony, in walked the farmer's wife and gave him a pile of paper, saying that she had forgotten to replace it that morning.

Even now, nearly sixty years later, we are still friends with some of those good people, including the woman who dropped her milk can in amazement when Dudley asked her in French at the roadside for some eggs for his mates. She exclaimed, "Good Lord, an English soldier who can speak French!"

I could tell you a lot more about the exciting things which we saw in Belgium and Holland, but I haven't got the time, unfortunately. During the fortnight we only stayed in two hotels. Although I was so young, the wonderful welcome and the kindness which we received will remain in my memory for ever. The "Entente Cordiale" was certainly alive at that time!

I'y avait enne p'tite affaire amusànte oprès qu'nous avait débartchi du baté en Guernési. Not biau moto, qu'avait fait parfaitement toute à travaers, mànquait ieune d'ses pougnies, et dé pusse son bounnet était plloin d'égrimaeures. Cor, mon père était bian guervaï et i'y avait enne vive distchutte atour qui serait réspaonsablle. L'ardjument dév'nait raide écauffaï, et tout d'aen caoup la p'tite vouaix du p'tit Jean interraonpit l'affaire. "Mais, pop, ch'est pas ichin not moto! Veyous-lé naote est pus llian dans l'rang". Pour saeure, i'y avait daeux Vauxhalls d'enne sorte et pouôinturaïs la mesme couleur, mais comme dé raisaon dauve des différents numéraos. Ch'tait ieune des d'ches occasiaons quànd lé simplle sens d'enn éfànt s'trouvit millaeux qu'la pus grànde counissànce des adultes. Hah! Nous rit acore atour chu moment-là tous les caoups qué tchique chaose nous fait y pensaïr.

There was an amusing little incident after we had disembarked from the boat in Guernsey. Our beautiful car, which had gone perfectly throughout, was missing one of its door handles, and furthermore its bonnet was covered in scratches. Cor, my father was very angry and there was a lively discussion about who would be responsible. The argument was becoming very heated, and all of a sudden the voice of little John interrupted things. "But, Dad, this isn't our car! See – ours is further along the line." Sure enough, there were two Vauxhalls of the same kind and painted the same colour, but naturally with different numbers. It was one of those occasions when the simple sense of a child was better than the greater knowledge of the adults. Hah! We still laugh about that moment every time something reminds us of it.

Enne Visite au Canada
par Robert Langlois

En dix-neuf chents saept mon gràn'père Henri Langlois (lé p'tit Harry du Paont à Torteval), dauve son frère Frederick et s'n'ami Ernest Sarre, pensirent qu'i voudraient aen p'tit d'avànture, et i décidirent dé s'en allaïr pour Canada. Les jonnes haommes avaient hardi d'l'affraont, parce qu'i n'avaient pas étaï tànt seulement en l'Anglléterre. Harry avait riocque dix-saept ans, mais, les v'là enroute dé Liverpool à bord du SS *Canada*. Laeux titchets dans la treisième classe coutaient daeux billes chaque - cor, la dépense!

J'n'ai pas gràn'ment d'détails dé chuque les treis gaillards faisaient là-bas. I trachirent du travas eiouque i pouvaient dans l'état d'Ontario, en utilisànt sàns doute laeux expérience sus la ferme et dans les spans. I visitirent l'Exhibitiaon Internationale à Toronto, et Harry travaillit pour aen p'tit temps dans énne manufacture d'sôlers. Il r'vint oprès daeux ans, chu caoup i viagit dans la daeuxième classe pour huit billes.

Nonànte-treis ans pus tard, l'affaire se répétit, car l'arrière p'tite fille dé Harry, ma fille Adèle, s'trouvit à Ontario étout. All'avait gogni aen 'scholarship' dé l'unniversitaïe dé Brock, qui fut noummaïe pour lé Guernésiais Sir Isaac Brock, qui sauvit lé Canada dé Haout en dix-huit chents douze quand les Ameritchens l'attachirent. Lé collège est situaï près du Loc Ontario. La régiaon a aen biau climat pour creitre les légeumes, et all'est bian counnaeuse comme 'lé gardin du Canada'.

A Visit to Canada
by Robert Langlois

In 1907 my grandfather Henry Langlois (little Harry of Le Pont, Torteval), his elder brother Frederick and a friend, Ernest Sarre thought they would like a bit of adventure, and they decided to go off to Canada. This was quite a bold thing to do, because they had not even been to England. Harry was only seventeen, but off they went from Liverpool on board the SS *Canada*. Their steerage tickets cost £2 each. What an expense!

I don't have many details of what the three lads got up to over there. They sought work wherever they could in the state of Ontario, no doubt using their experience on the farm and in the greenhouses. They visited the Toronto International Exhibition, and Harry worked for a time in a shoe factory. He returned after about two years, this time travelling second class for £8.

Ninety-three years later, history repeated itself, for Harry's great-granddaughter, my daughter Adèle, found herself in Ontario, too. She had been awarded a scholarship by Brock University, which was named after Guernseyman Sir Isaac Brock, who saved Upper Canada from the invading Americans in 1812. The campus is situated near Lake Ontario. The area enjoys a good climate for the growing of vegetables, and is well known as the 'garden of Canada'.

Lé meis d'aout en daeux milles ieune, j'fus par plane à Toronto, dauve ma faumme Elizabeth et mon fils Douglas, pour rencaontraïr l'Adèle, et nous fit aen tour par bus des gràndes villes dé l'est. Nous visitit la tac d'la Bataille dé Queenstown Heights, éiouque lé Général Brock perdit sa vie. La nâtiaon bâtit énne colaonne à sa memouaire, comme la sianne dé Nelson à Laondre mais tchiques pids pus haoute. Nous maontit les daeux chents cinquànte dégrais frànc au haout d'chu monument, et les tchurateurs étaient bian interêssis dé ouir qu'nous v'nait d'la pllache dé neissànce dé Brock.

Nous vit les magnifiques bâtiments du Parlément à Ottawa, des rivières plloines dé milliaons dé troncs d'arbres qui fllottaient enviaer la maïr, et la tour d'la télévisaon à Toronto, lé pus haout bâtiment du maonde. I'y'avait tout plloin d'fichu grànds courtis d'bllai - tout était si grànd!

La ville qu'nous oimait lè mux ch'tait Québec. All'est pus à la vieille mode, pas tànt d''skyscrapers'. Les citouoyens d'visaient lé Frànçais tout autouor d'naons, et tout était en daeux langages. J'epiyis dans l'almenas d'téléphaone, ét j'fus ravi d'découvrir qué Langlois était lé naom dé fomille quâsi lé pus coummun là-d'dans, surpâssaï riocque par Bouchard, un naom bian counnaeux en Jerri, j'pense.

I'y'avait réellement trop à veies durànt aen tchin'jours, mais nous raombillera jomais les spéctaclles dé Canada. Gràn'père raombillit pas nitou son temps dans chu pays memorablle, et i pâlait souvent d'ses expériences. Justément énne s'môine oprès qu'nous r'vint à la maisaon, nous aït caouse d'ête bian r'counnisànts, parce qué ch't'ait en chu temps-là qu'l'Amerique souffrit les attaques du aonze d'estembre.

In August 2001, I flew out to Toronto with my wife Elizabeth and son Douglas to join Adèle, and we took a coach tour of the main cities of the eastern region. We visited the site of the Battle of Queenstown Heights, where General Brock lost his life. The nation erected a column in his memory, similar to Nelson's Column in London, but several feet taller. We climbed the 250 steps to the top of this monument, and the curators were very interested to hear we came from Brock's birthplace.

We saw the magnificent parliament buildings of Ottawa, rivers filled with millions of logs being floated towards the sea, and the television tower in Toronto, the tallest building in the world. There was mile upon mile of huge fields of corn – everything was so big!

We liked the city of Quebec most of all. It is more traditional, with not so many skyscrapers. The citizens were speaking French all around us, and everything was in two languages. I looked through the telephone directory, and was surprised to find that Langlois was almost the most numerous family name in it, second only to Bouchard, which is a common name in Jersey, I think.

There was really too much to see in a mere fortnight, but we will never forget the sights of Canada. Grandfather did not forget his time in this memorable country either, and often talked about his experiences there. Just a week or so after getting home we had reason to be very thankful, because it was then that America suffered the attacks of 11th September 2001.

Chique j'frais si j'etais naufragit su en ile
par Helier d'Rocquoine (Helier Le Cheminant)

Etre naufragit su en ile d'mi a d'mi grandatte mai presente des problaime comparable au marriage. Nous entrons dans en nouvelle experience qui s'ra p'tetre difficile a s'ie ajustai. J'narais pas dautre accee a la bouanne soup q'ma maire faisait et, si j'avais auchunne esperance de survive s'rait seulement pas mais efforts personnel.

1   Tracherais pour d'yeau
Enne homme peut vivre des jours sans n'mangier mais pas sans n'bairre. J'd'gettrais pour des mouissons ou des animaux pour a guide. S'y a des animaux y'a d'yeau. Si y'a des guenons, y'a sans doute des cocquenattes, J'leu pelterais des rocques et i'm pelterais des cocquenattes et jerais a bairre et a mangier.

2   Pour mangeries
Apar de cocqyenattes, jerais acces a d'differants fruits sauvages et par d'jetai les animaux, jserais les quai qui s'rais pas enpouisouneua.

3   Pour protection
J'tracherais en cave ou j'bâtirais enne niche atour des caparie ramassai l'long du pioin. Et chi sait, nous i trouverait p'tetre bien d'che servisable ou utile. A morser corde amarai a an yaiche servirai d'line pour ligner ou pour faire en arc. Des fines bambou dauve an clliau dans l'but f'rait pour flache et s'rez bien muni pour la chase.

What I would do if I were shipwrecked on an island
by Helier d'Rocquoine (Helier Le Cheminant)

To be shipwrecked on a fairly large island presents me with problems comparable to marriage. We enter into a new experience to which it will be difficult to adjust. I would no longer have access to the good soup that my mother made, and if I had any hope of surviving it would only be because of my own efforts.

1   I would look for water
A man can live for days without eating but not without drinking. I would watch for birds or animals as a guide. If there are animals there is water. If there are monkeys there are no doubt coconuts. I would throw stones at them and they would throw coconuts at me, and I would have drink and food.

2   Food
Apart from coconuts, I would have access to different wild fruit and by watching the animals I would know which ones were not poisonous.

3   Protection
I would look for a cave or I would build a shelter with wreckage gathered along the high water mark. And who knows, I might find some very serviceable and useful things there. A piece of string tied to a binder could serve as a fishing line or to make a bow. Thin bamboos with a nail on the end would make an arrow and would be useful for hunting.

An morsait d'far comme en verte-velle pourait etre aduchit su en rocque et sevirait d'serper et nous s'servirait du fond d'bouteille pour allunai du feau. Des palle de bete s'raient utilisai pour hardes car, opres tout, biauquen y'at pas dautes gens su l'ile nous aumes a etre an p'tit rammassai....et i m'faudrait chique sorte de couverture pour diniet quand l'solel s'rait couchi. An moucher ou deau d'rocques aupres mon yiet d'fieilles prometrer d'ma a auceune bete qu'eprouveraient a m'attache.

4 En conclusion

Si j'ai ecapai les dangiers d'enne maïr cruelle i m'est possiblye de surmentai les problaime a terre dans en environment naturel en applichant la determination a la miette d'intelligence que j'possaide.

A piece of iron like a hinge could be sharpened on a rock and would serve as a chopper and we would use the bottom of a bottle to light a fire. Animal skins would be used for clothes for, after all, even though there are no other people on the island, we like to be a little covered up.... and I would need a covering for night-time when the sun has gone down. A heap or two of stones by my bed of leaves would threaten any animal that tried to attack me.

4 In conclusion

If I had escaped the dangers of a cruel sea it is possible for me to surmount the problems on land in a natural environment on adding determination to the little intelligence that I possess.

Enn courte visite
par Helier le Cheminant (Helier d'Rocquoine)

La terre etait bllanche dauve enn courtrpointe de neis, et le vent mordai dauve des dents qui perchais l'travar des hardes d'aen jaune haumme perdu et errant dans enn fuorest.

La vaëu dans la f'nait'e d'enn p'tite cabane dans aen cllergissemnet fut pour li comme aen soupir de vie – comme la bracq du ciel.

Gervelant d'fraid et affomaï comme enn fuaïe, i tapi a l'us. L'us ouvri, et aen viar haumme se pllanti dans l'ouverture.

"Chiq' tu veur?" l'y d'mandi l'viar. Le jaune haumme l'y caonti san predicament dans chiqu' paroles et pllaidi pour d'l'abri pour la niet, enn bouchie a mangiait et la chance de s'ecauffaï. Le viar le fis entraï. Le jaune haumme halli sa grosse cotte et s'mis a frottaï et soufflaï dans sais moins.

"Pourchi q'tu fais chenna?" l'y d'mandi l'viar.

"Pour les cauffaï et encouragiai la cirtchulatiaön dans mes deights," repouni le jaune haumme.

" Eh bian, assiait te a la tablle et j'te dounn'rai enn bouane caude bowlaïe d'soupe de navaeis."

L'jaune haumme le r'mercyi et s'assyevi, et le viar y fouri enn grosse bowlaïe d'vant l'musset. Auprais avai emyounnaï du poin dans la soupe, le jaune haumme an prins enn tchulraïe et s'mis a soufflaï d'su la soupe d'vant la mangier.

"Pourchi q'tu fais chenna?" l'y d'mandi l'viar.

"Pour la refraidgait," repouni l'jaune haumme.

A short visit

by Helier LeCheminant (Helierd'Rocquoine)

The ground was white with a covering of snow, and the wind bit with teeth that pierced through the clothes of a young man lost and wandering in a forest.

The light in the window of a little cabin in a clearing was for him like a breath of life – the gateway to heaven.

Shivering with cold and ravenous, he knocked on the door. The door opened and an old man stood in the opening..

"What do you want?" the old man asked him. The young man explained his predicament in a few words and pleaded to have some shelter for the night, a mouthful to eat and the chance to warm himself. The old man bade him enter. The young man took off his overcoat and began to rub and blow on his hands.

"Why are you doing that?" the old man asked him.

"To warm them and to encourage the circulation back into my fingers," replied the young man.

" Well, sit at the table and I'll give you a good hot bowl of turnip soup."

The young man thanked him and sat at the table, and the old man thrust a big bowl of soup in front of his nose. After he had crumbled some bread into the soup, the young man took a spoonful and began to blow on the soup before eating it.

"Why are you doing that?" the old man asked him.

"To cool it," replied the young man.

Le viar fut marri, il aggripi sa hache q'etait dans aen coin, an furie, l'y dis "Quand t'as entraï, t'as soufflaï dans tes moins pour les ecauffaï; aucht'aüre tu soufflé su ta soupe pour la refraidgait. Chiq'un qui peut soufflaï caud et fraid dauve laëux bouche sont sorchier! Cllange te ou j'tai fendrai an daëux dauve ma hache!"

L'jaune haumme se butti vite, tchulbuti sa chaire, aggripi sa cotte q'etai pendue su aen crocq et s'ecapi par l'us vite comme sais dgerais pouvais l'portaï.

The old man became angry, snatched up his axe which was in a corner and, in a fury, said to him, "When you came in, you blew on your hands to warm them; now you blow on your soup to cool it. Someone who can blow hot and cold with their mouth is a sorcerer. Clear off or I'll split you in two with my axe!"

The young man stood up quickly, knocked over his chair, snatched his coat from a hook and escaped through the door as fast as his legs could carry him.

Le Georges fut effrais
par Marjorie Ozanne

Y'a bian d's aunnai y'avait en viar fosseux au Valle. Enne jounas i s'trouvit enne fosse à faire, mais il avait étai ardi enbarrassai, et i s'decidit d'la faire par le fin de la leune. Al'tait au pioin et vaiout comme jour.

La fosse était dans le shimtiaire de l'eglise, du cotaid'la mialle, a daitre en amontens, et pas dai yan d'la hêche. Quaën la fosse était deviar quatre pie et d'mi en avers, i oui des pas d'vallai avaux le shmin.

Sh'tait le Georges Mairmignier qu'avait étai condire sa garse qui d'meurait auprais le Gren Fort. Il allai terjous le travas du shimtiaire en s'en v'nent pour racourshier sen shmin.

Le viar fosseux epyi par le bord d'la fosse, et criyit, "Oyous, pouvous vais quai haire qu'il est?"

Le Georges se d'virit et vit enne bianche taite (et le bianche smoque que le viar mettait) denishier de d'dans enne fosse. I prie la fouite avaux le shmin, mais pour empyerier l'affaire, le viar sautit de d'dans la fosse et s'enfuit souvente de li, criyant, "Naiyai pas peux, sh'est mai, sh'est mai."

Le paure Georges r'gardit derriaire li.et vu l'apparition qui le suivait. I volit par su la hêche, et pour sie-li comme si l'avait étai suivi par le viar nar.

Le fosseux dit à men paire autouor, et comme i dit, " Le paure jaunne houme, mais ai-ti peux, j'en avais-ju r'gré." Men paire se mis à rire. I trouvait shenna bian drole, et comme i dit, "J'crai bian qu'il allait à grèns pas, et il est bian yian s'i va terjous!"

George had a fright
by Marjorie Ozanne

Many years ago, there was an old grave-digger in the Vale. One day he found that he had a grave to dig, but he had been very busy and so he decided to dig it by the light of the moon. It was full and we could see as if by day.

The grave was in the cemetery of the church, on the side of the lowland, on the right on a slope, and not too far from the gate. When the grave was about four and a half feet deep, he heard some footsteps coming down the path.

It was George Mairmignier who had been escorting his girlfriend home to where she lived near to the Grand Fort. He always went across the cemetery coming back to shorten his journey.

The old grave-digger peered over the edge of the grave and called, " Hey, can you see what time it is?"

George turned round and saw a white head (and the white smock the old man wore) emerging out of a grave. He took to his heels down the path, but to make matters worse, the old man jumped out of the grave and went off after him, shouting, "Don't be afraid, it's me, it's me."

Poor George looked behind him and saw the apparition that followed him. He leapt over the gate and ran home as if the devil was following him.

The grave-digger told my father about it, and he said, "The poor young man, wasn't he frightened, I was so sorry for him." My father began to laugh. He found that very funny, and as he said, "I'm sure that he took big steps and he'll be a long way off if he's still going!"

Le Jean et l'Pierre au paison
par Marjorie Ozanne

Le Jean et l'Pierre avaient holidais. I'n savaient pas tchi faire pour passai l'temps, et ils taient enniais. Su la fin leux maire die, "Pourchi qu'vous n'allais pas au paison? Vous soulaites y allai l'aunnas passi et vous avaites en des temps de bouannes paiques."

" Mais vaire," s'fie l'Jean, "nous era p'taites tenserment ën fricot pour l'ca."

Les v'la allai pour la banque dauve enne fourque et ën tin pour trashier d'la baite. I d'meuraient a Rocquoine, i n'avaient pas yan a allai.

Bientôt les v'la assis su l'but d'la p'tite caushie et dans p'ti temps ils avaient enne baille p'tite paique. Tout d'ën cau le Pierre oui enne equavinnie. Le Jean etait dans yaux. Il avait slipai su du vraic; par bounheur qui pouvait nouai.

Les v'la allai pour la maison. Le Jean restit su l'pas et l'Pierre fut trashier sa maire. "Vous piais t'i v'ni," s'fie ti, "le Pierre n'pouvait pas attrapai l'paison vite assai, qui fait il a sautai a la maire pour allai l'queure, et il est trop mouyi pour entrai."

John and Peter go fishing
by Marjorie Ozanne

John and Peter were on holiday. They didn't know what to do, and they were bored. At last their mother said, "Why don't you go fishing? You used to go last year and you had good catches sometimes."

"Oh yes," said John, "we may even get a feed for the cat."

So off they went to the beach with a fork and a tin to look for bait. They lived at Rocquaine, so they didn't have far to go.

Soon they were sitting on the end of the little pier and in a very short time they had a nice little catch. Suddenly Peter heard a splash. John was in the water. He had slipped on some seaweed; thank goodness he could swim.

They went home. John stayed on the doorstep and Peter went to look for his mother. "Will you please come," he said, "Peter couldn't catch a fish fast enough so he jumped in the water to fetch it, and he is too wet to come in."

L'esprit du Haut d'la Varde
par Marjorie Ozanne

I n'est pas terjous seriaux, et parce qu'il est en vrai esprit Guernesais, il est tout a fait probable qui prend part dans bien des shensons a bouannes opportunitais.

Par example! En jour quen i tchaiyait d'la nais, en viar haomme etait su la miaille a ramassai ses biches qu'etaient fiquies au pid d'la Varde. I oui enne vouaix recitait shais laine ishain,

> "Les Français qui piement leux ouais
> Craquent leux puches et les font quais."

Quand i r'gardit de waique la vouaix v'nait, n'y avait persaonne a vais. I fut print d'grand peux, et s'n'allait pour la maison aussi vite comme i pouvait, mais d'vens qui n'vainre au but d'la miaille en corbin passit volant. Au meme temps le viar oui la meme vouaix qui disai,

> "Corbin, corbin ta maison brule,
> Va t'en tcheure ten poin et burre.
> J'ai la cllaie dans ma paute
> Jaumais tu la vairras daute."

Le paure viar, bien effras, print a ses talons, et n'perdit pas d'temps a gaugner sie li. I n'er fut jaumais a la miaille au sar.

The spirit from the top of the Varde
by Marjorie Ozanne

It is not always serious, and because it is a true Guernsey spirit, it is entirely probable it takes part in many songs at every opportunity.

For example! One day when snow was falling, an old man was on the lowlands fetching his goats which were tethered at the foot of the Varde. He heard a voice reciting these lines,

> "The French who pluck their geese
> Crack their fleas and let them fall."

When he looked round to see where the voice came from, there was no-one to be seen. He was seized by great fear, and was going home as fast as he could, but before he came to the end of the lowlands a crow came flying by. At the same time the old man heard the same voice which said,

> "Crow, crow your house is burning,
> Go and fetch your bread and butter.
> I have the key in my pocket
> Never will you see it again."

The poor old man, terrified, took to his heels and didn't waste any time getting home. He never went back to the lowlands in the evening.

Shu qui s'arrivit a la ville
par Marjorie Ozanne

En Samedi matin, la ville etait comme de couteume pionne de monde, tout etait bien trequille. Y'en avait a shuppai, d'autes a s'ente d'visai ou a gardai dans les f'netes.

Tout d'en cau, v'la en jaunne piens, courant amont l'Polai, et dans dau minutes n'en v'la enne aute. S'fie l'sian en d'vans, "Vien vite, il disent qu'il a quais dans la cauchie," et les v'la allai avaux la Grens rue au gallo.

Dans quiques minutes, y'en avait enne rabyas qui couorait souvent de yaux, et par le temps qui vinrent au coin de l'Arcade, la rue etait pionne de gens qui couorair envier l'eglise d'la ville. Au qu'uns n'savaient pour chi qui couorar ni waique i s'n allaient, et un policeman qu'epprouvait a l's aretai fut abbatu dans la rue, et s'trouvit assis su les pas d'la banque.

I couorais comme des troubais, les siens qui n'se bougais pas etaient assis par la rue. Quens les deux poupains qui m'naient la rabyas vinrent auprais la cauchie, i furent jusque'au bord et epyirent dans l'havre.

"La," s'firent ti, "les v'la, les v'la."

Dans daux minutes le bord d'la cauchie etait pion d'monde. Il n'navait qu'a sente poussaie dans la cauchie, et tout shu qui virent sh'tai en batai dauve en bienche couleur, et en grend naires letters, il tait mi APRIL FOOL.

What happened in Town
by Majorie Ozanne

One Saturday morning, the town was full of people as usual, everything was peaceful. There were those who were shopping, others were talking to each other or looking in the shop windows.

Suddenly, there were two young fellows running up the Pollet, and in two minutes, there was another. Said the one in front, "Come quickly, they say that he has fallen in the dock," and they were off down the High Street at the gallop.

In a few minutes, there was a mob running after them, and by the time they came to the corner of the Arcade, the street was full of people who were running towards the Town church. No one knew why they were running nor where they were going, and a policeman who tried to stop them was knocked down in the street, and found that he was sitting on the steps of the bank.

They ran like madmen, the ones who didn't move were sitting in the street. When the two idiots who led the rabble came near to the quay, they went right to the edge and peered into the harbour.

"There," they said, "there they are, there they are."

In two minutes the edge of the quay was full of people. They were nearly pushing each other into the dock, and all that they saw was a boat with a white flag, and in big black letters it said APRIL FOOL.

L'Henri tchi s'en fut au Canada
par E M Renouf

Ch'tait pas p'tête q'il avait tant d'manjue es pids coum i'voulai veis pus llian qui fit Henri s'decidaie d'allaïr au Canada. I'd'mandis a l'Emilie tchique a'l en crayais, ch'tait enne bouanne garce et all'tait bien d'avis d'allai dauve li et d'veis tchique en etait d'ches cougns la. Su la fin i'vint l'jour d's'n allai d'Guernesi. Y'avait dáeux s'moine a gagnier franc a l'aute cotai du Canada dans tcheis temps la, mais i'faessait bel et i'veire tout plloin d'tchaie.

I'l arrivire tout entier et l'bouan but en hàout. Y'avait d's etais qu'il en fricachaie, epis l'hiver d'la neis hàout coum le col. Au matin l's oeus tchjitiae dans la poèle coum des galoats. I'l taés jonne et i'l'avais tous plloin du plaissi mais n'y'avait pas d'souain ouecqe i'l taés i's'entre d'vissait terjous en Guernesiais.

En jour i'vint des nouvelles q'les Allemand avais c'menchi a r'faire l'aeurs gestes. L'Henri en etait gesnai, i' counnissai leux gré d'avant mais n'y'avait pas grand tchose qui pouvait y faire. Oprès en p'tit i'oui-dire qu'il taés en Guernesi. J'vous d'mande si'il'tait en fôuaïe d'pensair qu'ditai empîatre etais a pilvaudaïr et empestaïr sen p'tit Guernesi. I'fut si guervaï que i's'en fut tout dret listaïe.

Quand i's trouvi la il'y d'mandirent quai age q'il avai, mais l'paure Henri n'etait pas dautre si jonne coum il avait etai. Chena failli a'l tchulbutáir, mais il'tait entrinaï coum en âne et i'n s'avisi mafait pas daeux caups a menti. Su la fin le v'la assermentai et plléchi dauve dautre Canadians dans aën regiment d'Ecossais.

Eh bien, j'vous d'mande si l'en v'la aën biaou pitchet, v'la donc Henri aën Guernesiais, et aën Vallais, dauve des Canadians, et gráïe en Ecossais. Si les Allemands avais bian seux, tchai assai pour les faire tous fichier l'camp pour cie aïeux.

Henry who went off to Canada
by E M Renouf

Perhaps it was that he had itchy feet and that he wanted to see more (of the world) that made Henry decide to go to Canada. He asked Emily what she thought, she was a good lass and she was keen to go with him to see what it was like in those parts. At last the day came to leave Guernsey. It took a fortnight to reach the other side of Canada in those days, but the weather was good and they saw many things.

They arrived safe and sound. There were some summers that were boiling hot (they fried), then in winter there was snow as up to their necks. In the morning the eggs thrown into the pan were like pebbles. They were young and they had a lot of fun but it didn't matter where they were, they always spoke Guernsey-French to each other.

One day news came that the Germans had begun to make threats again. Henry was frightened, he knew their intentions from before but there was not much that he could do about it. After a little while he heard that they were in Guernsey. I ask you if he was in a rage to think that such oafs were trampling on and polluting his little Guernsey. He was so angry that he went to enlist straight away.

When he got there, they asked him how old he was, but poor Henry was not as young as he used to be. That almost upset his plan, but Henry was as obstinate as a donkey and he certainly didn't think twice about lying. At last he was sworn in and placed with other Canadians in a Scottish regiment.

Well I ask you if this was a fine pickle, there was Henry a Guernseyman and a Vale man, with Canadians, and dressed as a Scotsman. If the Germans had known, it was enough to make them clear off back home.

I's doubtai en p'tit qu'il y baillirent des cotilläons, mais nou-fait il'y baillirent des brais aurun. Chena l'fit fiaër pasqué ses genouaï n'tais pas trop biaous, et i croiniet p'tête tchique journas d'tcheies assis a tchu plat dans enne troque d'ortie. En finissant il' y cllapeire aën grand bounnet Ecossais su l'hàout d'la tête, il'tait si grànd qu'il y tcheisiais franc par dessus l's oreilles, ch'tait tchuque il'applais, en rislaïe, enne coueme.

S'n affaire allai bian assais, y avait enne amas d'frigadians et d'soudarts de toute les sorte la ouecque il'tait. En Samedi i's'n allaïr y avait enne grànde assembllaïe de tous, et il'taits pour marchier à travaers la ville. Toute la campogne s'trouvi pour veis tchuque i's'passait.

Les frigadians etais les prumier, et l'regiment du Henri l'perchain, i marchire franc d'en but d'la ville a l'autre, et r'tournire par enne autre route la ouecque il'avais c'menchi. L'Emilie et leûx fille Adele etais arrêtair pour li, et tous les bougeais enviàrs le milli d'la ville, les marchépid etait tout plloin.

L'Henri aver tout plloin d'tchiai a lu dire et d'vissait bouan réde en Guernesiais. Quand il'arrivaieres a aën quatre carrefour i' fallait arrêtair pour traversair la route et Henri r'gardi d'cotaï pour d'mandaie es faummes par ouecque i'voulais allai. I' faillit en tcheies quand i'voie qu'il avait marchi aën but de chemin dauve enne autre faumme qui n'counnissais pas en tout, et y avait bèrdangui en Guernesiais.

Si nous avait veue l'r'gard qu'a li bailliet, a'n avait mafait pas enne belle encornoëure, et Henri, qui n'tait puis en tout d'humeur d'avait du broue, il'erait bien mux oimair enne bouanne goutte. Quand i's'viri bord pour bord, pour ag'vair tout, i' viet l'Emilie et l'Adele qui marchez en p'tit en derriere, i'vaiees tous tchuque i's'passait et en avais aën foutu pliassi. Eh bien, i'dise qui vaux mûx en rire q'd'en braire, et il'en on rit bien des caups d'pres.

He was a little worried that they would give him petticoats (a kilt), but no, they gave him some trousers instead. That pleased him because his knees were not too attractive, and he was afraid that perhaps one of these days he would fall sitting down on his backside in a bed of nettles. In finishing they thrust a large Scottish bonnet on top of his head, it was so big that it fell right down over his ears, it was what he called, jokingly, a cow-pat.

He managed well enough, there were a lot of sailors and soldiers of all kinds where he was. On Saturday there was going to be a great assembly of everyone and they were going to march through the town. Everyone came to see what was happening.

The sailors were the first, and Henry's regiment was next, they marched from one end of the town to the other, and returned by another route to where they had started from. Emily and their daughter Adèle were waiting for him, and everyone moved towards the centre of town, the pavements were so full.

Henry had a lot of things to tell them and was talking away in Guernsey-French. When they arrived at a crossroads they had to wait to cross the road and Henry looked round to ask the women which way they wanted to go. He nearly fell down when he saw that he had walked part of the way with another woman whom he didn't know at all, and had chatted to her in Guernsey-French.

If we had seen the look she gave him, she certainly didn't have a lovely appearance, and Henry, who wasn't in the mood to have any trouble, would have preferred a good drink. When he turned round, to make matters worse, he saw Emily and Adèle who were walking a little behind, they saw all that was happening and were having a blooming good laugh. Well, they say that it's better to laugh than to cry, and they have laughed about it many times.

Alfred va au païssaön
par Tom Renouf (Tom du Camp du Roi)

Aen jour des païssöunier son allair au païssaïon et ils d'mandair a
Alfred si voulier allair d'aive iaeux. Alfred did oui et il furent pour
le Grand Havre. Ils sen allant enviaer le vouest de l'ile, et y'avait
enne bonne breeze.

Alfred se trouvi par trot bien et il c'merchi a etre malade. Il
s'endormice dans le faond du baté dans le temps qui petcher le
païssaön. Ils hoalair le païssaön dans le baté en raond d'Alfred. Il
en avait autour du visage quand ils etais finir.

Quand ils fait le passage pour le Grand Havre la brise avait
bein abatau.Quand Alfred mais ses pies sur la sabllaon il etais
bien.

Alfred jomais fut dans enn petit baté. Quand il arrivais a la
maisson le grànpère d'mandair s'il avait iaeu aen böuan jour. Alfred
c'menchier a rire, et il did malade le jour.

36

Alfred goes fishing
by Tom Renouf (Tom du Camp du Roi)

One day some fishermen were going fishing and they asked Alfred if he wanted to go with them. Alfred said yes and they went off to Grand Havre. They were going towards the west of the island, and there was a good breeze.

Alfred did not feel too well and he began to be sick. He fell asleep in the bottom of the boat during the time that they were catching the fish. They threw the fish down around Alfred. He had some around his face when they were finished.

When they were on passage to Grand Havre the breeze had abated quite a lot. When Alfred put his feet on the sand he was better.

Alfred never went in a small boat again. When he arrived at home grandfather asked if he had had a good day. Alfred began to laugh and said (that he) was sick all day.

Le Grànpère et les ormés
par Tom Renouf (Tom du Camp du Roi)

Le grànpère vouller allair es ormés et il d'mandair a ses deux fils Joe et Alfred pour allair d'auve li. Ils furent a Bordeaux et ils avais en fricot* chatchun.

Aen jour Alfred se decidi de sassieis su les rocques pour veies ouecque les paissounier avais laeur ormés. La perchoin maraies qui furent es ormés Alfred s'assievi su les rocques es r'gardair le grànpère et Joe allair.

Quand ils r'venir et r'gardair le ponier de Alfred il n'avait rian. Mais Alfred s'butti quand les paissounnier arrivair. Il les suivait ils furent pa longue temps parti et asvais des ormés. La perchoin maraies Alfred dit au grànpère de le siere et il asais des ormés dans bien petit temps.

---

* Aen fricot: enough for a 'feed', a meal

Grandpa and the ormers
by Tom Renouf (Tom du Camp du Roi)

Grandpa wanted to go ormering and he asked his two sons Joe and Alfred to go with him. They went to Bordeaux and caught a feed each.

One day, Alfred decided to sit on the rocks to see where the fishermen had their ormers. The next tide when they went ormering, Alfred sat on the rocks and watched Grandpa and Joe go off.

When they came back and looked in Alfred's basket, he had nothing. But Alfred stood up when the fishermen arrived. He followed them. They were not gone very long and had some ormers. The next tide, Alfred told Grandpa and Joe to follow him and they had some ormers in a very short time.

Le Granpère se d'mente d'la j'las
par Li meme (Tom Renouf. Tom du Camp du Roi)

Nos gens etaient terjous a acatai d'la j'las des shoppes. Vous compernais le gardin etait pioin de frit, des frases j'usques es preune. En dire la veritai, y'en avait assai pour tous les Taudevine, comme nous dit parfais. Nous erait peux faire des pottas de j'las.

Mais creyons que nos gens prendaient shette poine la? Mafe nenain. Tout la j'las que nous mangeait etait pret fait, du boucas qu'n'avait pas de r'lais. Ils taient vraiment trop fenians pour leux mettres a la faire.

Enne journas j'prins couorage et leux die, "Pourqui don que vous faisai poui nne miette de j'las. Y'avais franbouaise, frase, et guerouaiseau dans le gardin. La Louise ete moyenment roueitre shu jour la et a m'die d'enne vouaix tout ragoine, "Veyous si vous avais envie de d'quai d'meme faisi le bravement vous meme."

Quique j'pouvais dire. Quel shanse qu'en pauvre viar a dire enne parole? Qui fait j'me tau ou bien j'erais yeux enne autre goulas, et pour en dire la veritai l'affaire n'en vallait pas la poine.

Mais arretai empti, le viar n'est pas si ait comme ils ont l'idee, et enne aunnas quen de couteume j'pensit qu'il tait temps de en d'mentai. Toinias de mequir, nous en avait honnait de vais le frit comme shenna.

Enne arlevas pour tais la Louise ouvrist enne nouvelle pottas de j'las d'la shoppe comme de raison. La meme serras quen nos gens etaient partis a l'assembias, j'vit ma shense de laux jouais justement enne belle petite gaume. J'romigit dans la pouque a shiques et j'trouvit en biaux p'tit morce de rouge et bianche shiques indiaunne a peupre le size de la mointi d'en moucheux de paoute.

J'print la p'tit shique dans la cuissine et la fourrit la miyi de la pottas de j'las.

Grandfather interferes with the jam
by Himself (Tom Renouf. Tom du Camp du Roi)

Our family always bought jam from the shops. You'll understand that the garden was full of fruit, from strawberries to plums. To tell the truth there was enough for 'all the Tostevins' , as we say sometimes. We could have made pots and pots of jam.

But do you think that our family would take all that trouble? Not likely! All the jam we ate was ready made, stuff that had no taste. They were truly too lazy to get on with making some.

One day, I took courage and told them, "Why don't you set to and make a little bit of jam?" There were raspberries, strawberries and gooseberries in the garden. Louise was fairly crabby that day and she said to me in a very argumentative voice "Look if you fancy that kind of thing, go on and make it yourself."

What could I say. What chance has a poor old man to say a word? So I kept quiet or else I would have had another mouthful, and to tell the truth, it wasn't worth the bother.

But wait a bit, the old man is not as stupid as they think and one year as usual I thought that it was time to do something about it. Darn it, we were ashamed to see the fruit like that.

One afternoon, for tea Louise opened a new pot of jam from the shop of course. The same evening when the family had gone to a meeting, I saw my chance to play a little game on them. I rummaged about in the rag bag and I found a lovely little piece of red and white calico rag about the size of half a pocket handkerchief.

I took the little rag into the kitchen and pushed it into the middle of the pot of jam.

☛

Le lendemain, quen j'etaimes a avait notre tais la Louse fourit s'en coutai dans la j'las et a die, aupres y'avait fougounnai pour enne ashee, "Oyous y'a quiquechose de drole dans la j'las." En meme temps a hallit la shique.

"La donc," j'y die, "i pari que quique pauvre misarable qui etait a faire la j'las coupit s'en de et pit perdit sa shique parmi la j'las. Tu peu vais qu'a lest tout taquies de sang."

Je vous dirai pas tique la Louse die, mais a na jaumais acatai d'j'las des shoppes depie, et le frit dans le gardin est terjous sauvai auchetaire.

Next day, when we were having our tea Louise put her knife into the jam and she said, after having poked about for ages, "Hang on, there's something funny in the jam." At the same time she took out the rag.

"There now," I said to her, "it looks as if some poor wretch who was making the jam cut his finger and then lost his bandage in the jam. You can see that it is all blood stained."

I won't tell you what Louise said, but she has never bought jam from the shop since, and the fruit in the garden is always saved these days.

Le Service de la Moissaon
par Tom Renouf (Tom du Camp du Roi)

A aen egllise en Angleterre ils etais a celebrair la moissaon d'auve des biau services le Demanche. Le Lundi au saer y've le soupai d'la moissaon. Le ministre et sa Daume etain a aigue a preparair le soupair que tous l'apprecais

Opres le r'pas ils avait la vente du produit. Opres la vente le Ministre et sa Daume etais a aigue a les members de l'egllise a cllergir et a lavair les vessets. Ils restire opres mignet a finir de cllergir. Il etait bian douze haeures et demi d'lavant avait mit tout en ordre, et le ministre et sa Daume quitteir de l'egllise pour a maisaon.

Quand ils etait pour le lliate la Daume du ministre ditte que a l'avais mal a la tete, et a r'gardait pour sa empoutcher. A dit a les a l'egllise. Le ministre dit, "J'men vais la tcheure a l'egllise pour que tes les tablets." Le Ministre, dans ses pyjamas, prendre le motor et fut pour l'egllise.

Aen r'gardair a l'egllise les vaeux etais acore allumai, et il fut dans l'egllise pour matte les vaeux hors. Il etait a lotcher l'hus et il strouvi dans les bras de daeux policemaen qui vouller savouaer qu'il tai a faire.

Le Ministre expllicher que sa daume avait rembillair sa empoucher a l'egllise. Le police le die qu'il avait a allair au Police Station. Le Ministre telephone a sa Daume pour dire qu'il avait a restair a la station pour la gniet.

Le Ministre dormir bien, et il laeu aen boun dejeunai, du lard et des oeues au matin, et il fue pour la maisaon. Le Demanche le ministre dis la caonte a sa congregatian, et ils tous mis a rire de bouan tchoeur.

The Harvest Service
by Tom Renouf (Tom du Camp du Roi)

At a church in England they were celebrating Harvest Festival with some lovely services on the Sunday. On the Monday evening there was the Harvest Supper. The minister and his wife were helping to prepare the supper which everyone appreciated.

After the meal they had the sale of produce. After the sale the minister and his wife were helping the members of the church to clear and wash the dishes. They stayed until after midnight to finish clearing up. It was well after half past twelve before everything was in order, and the minister and his wife left the church to go home.

When they were ready for bed, the minister's wife said that she had a headache, and she looked for her bag. She said that it was at the church. The minister said, "I'm going to fetch it from the church so that you will have your tablets." The minister, in his pyjamas, took the car and went to the church.

When he looked at the church, the lights were still lit, so he went into the church to turn them off. He was locking the door when he found himself in the arms of two policemen who wanted to know what he was doing.

The minister explained that his wife had forgotten her bag at the church. The police told him that he would have to go to the Police Station. The minister telephoned his wife to tell her that he had to stay at the station for the night.

The minister slept well and he had a good breakfast of bacon and eggs in the morning, and he went home On Sunday, the minister told the tale to his congregation, and they all started to laugh heartily.

William et son gràn'père
par Tom Renouf (Tom du Camp du Roi)

Aen jour le gràn'père de William li demandi sil iré au pond d'auve li. Quand il marchier envair le pond y'avais aen shoppe de deuxieme main qui avais des livres a vendre. Le gran'père se tournair a William et li dit," Ch'est l'histouare du monde."

Le gràn'père oimair terjour a lliere.

"Men portairé tu aen livre, et j'portairé lautre," il demandi. William li dit oui.

"Ch'est des grand epais livre; mais les lliere pas a travaers." demandi William.

"J'menvais eprouvair," dit le gràn'père. Ils fut dans la shoppe. Le gràn'père acatai les deux livres. Ils marchier pour la maisaon, mai le William trouvais le sien b'sànt.

La gràn'mère regardair quand ils marchier dans la maisaon.

"Eh bian," s'fit le gràn'père, "il faudra retournair pour le pond." V'la le gràn'père et William alais. Le gràn'père fut dans la shoppe pour acatair sa viande, aupres dans la shoppe a papier pour la Gazette. Au sortant de la shoppe le gràn'père regardair enviars l'hologe.

"L'ou, v'la Nico Rihoy c'arrivair d'auve sen baté. Faout allair veis s'il a du paissaon." Les v'la allair. Mais oui, il avais des houvlins et des chancres. S'fit le gràn'père a William, " Tu dira a tes gens qui faux q'vous v'naiz pour le thée desmanche."

Le gràn'père demandair a Nico le pris pour le pus gros chancre; deaux ch'lins six penni. Le gràn'père et William allair pour la maisaon. Quand il entrais, le gràn'père dit a la gràn'mère, "Nous sont va avais d'la visite pour le thée desmanche. William dira a ses gens pour v'nir pour le thée. V'e tu, jé aportai le pus gros chancre que Nico avais."

William and his grandpa

by Tom Renouf (Tom du Camp du Roi)

One day, William's grandpa asked him if he would go to the Bridge with him. When he walked towards the Bridge there was a second-hand shop which had books for sale. Grandpa turned to William and said to him, "It's the history of the world."

Grandpa always liked to read.

"Would you carry a book for me and I will carry the other?" he asked him. William said yes.

"They are big thick books, but you don't read them right through?" asked William.

"I'm going to try," said Grandpa. They went into the shop. Grandpa bought the two books. They walked towards the house, but William found his heavy.

Grandma looked at them when they walked into the house.

"Well," said Grandpa," we must go back to the Bridge." Off Grandpa and William went. Grandpa went into the shop to buy his meat and afterwards to the paper shop for the Gazette. On leaving the shop, Grandpa looked towards the clock tower.

"Oh there is Nico Rihoy arriving in his boat. Let's go and see if he has some fish." Off they went. Yes, he had some spider crabs and some chancres (crabs). Said Grandpa to William, "You'll tell your folks that they must come to tea on Sunday."

Grandpa asked Nico the price of the biggest chancre; two shillings and sixpence. So off went Grandpa and William back home. When they entered the house, Grandpa said to Grandma, "We are going to have people to tea on Sunday. William will tell his folks to come to tea. Look, I've brought the biggest chancre that Nico had."

Les patchet d'la Red Cross
par Gerald O Robilliard

Les Guernésiais qu'étaient restai dans l'île de Guernesi durant l'otchupatiaon des Allemands s'rant terjours r'counnissant à la Red Cross pour aver arrangi le baté *Vega* pour apportai les vivres et les medicaments quand le maonde de Guernesi était dans l'grand besougn. Le prumier viage du *Vega* arrivit le meis d'janvier 1944 dauve sét chents chinquante touniaux de vivres. Ch'tait quate meis d'vant la Libératiaon.

Le démanche, le maonde était d'mandai de r'cllamai aen patchet d'la Red Cross en produissant laeux livre de ratiaons. Y avait quasi chinq ans qu'les Guernésiais n'avaient pas vaeux de bouannes c'mmoditais comme chena. Y avait des tinnais d'paissaon, d'la croime, du lait, du chucre, du burre et mesme du chocolat. Mais les Guernésiais étaient r'counnissants. Le maonde avait étai djerni d'gardai les patchets muchi car les Allemands étaient si mal nourri qu'i pourraient bian éprouvai à les volai.

Le Charlie et la Sophie avaient étai tcheur les patchets dauve laeux bikes. Quand i passirent la battrie ès Laurens, y avait enne djene de soudars Allemands qui les virent dauve les patchets. Charlie avait r'merchi qu'ils les r'gardaient vaillantment.

Le Charlie et la Sophie allaient tous les demanches à l'église, mais comme s'fit Charlie, "Je m'en vais restai à la maisaon à ces sé. J'croins qu'les patchets sés volais. Sophie dit "Ch'est la enne boaunne idée," et a s'en fut pour l'église. Charlie resti à la maisaon. Ils avaient couterme, que quand i sortaient, il'allumaient enne p'tite laempe à huile dans l'porta pour faire à craire qu'ils'taient à la maisaon.Quand i sortaient, pour n'prende pas la cllai d'la maisaon, i la mettaient dans la bouatte à lattres.

The parcels from the Red Cross
by Gerald O Robilliard

The Guernsey people who were left behind on the island of Guernsey during the occupation by the Germans will always be grateful to the Red Cross for having arranged for the ship *Vega* to bring foodstuffs and medicines when the population of Guernsey was in such great need. The first load of the *Vega* arrived in the month of January 1944 with seven hundred and fifty tons of foodstuffs. It was four months before the Liberation.

On the Sunday, the population was asked to claim a parcel from the Red Cross on producing their ration books. It was almost five years since the Guernsey people had seen good foodstuffs like that. There were tins of fish, cream, milk, sugar, butter and even some chocolate. How grateful the Guernsey people were. The population had been warned to keep the parcels hidden because the Germans were so badly nourished that they could easily try to steal them.

Charlie and Sophie had been to fetch the parcels with their bikes. When they passed the gun emplacement at Les Laurens there was a crowd of German soldiers who saw the parcels. Charlie had noticed that they were watching them closely.

Charlie and Sophie went to church every Sunday, but as Charlie said, "I'm going to stay at home this evening. I'm afraid that the parcels could be stolen." Sophie said, "That's a good idea," and she went off to church. Charlie stayed at home. Usually, when they went out, they lit a little oil lamp in the hall to make believe that they were at home. When they left, so as not to take the key of the house with them, they put it in the letter-box.

Charlie ouit des pas et i pensit, "Y a chiqu'un à rodai. J'crais bian que ch'est des Allemands." Il'tait abas dans l'portas et i vit enne moin à travars la bouatte à lattres. A n'pouvait pas trouvai la cllai pasqué a n'tait pas là. Charlie aeut la presence d'esprit qu'il avait mit l'pokeur dans l'faeu.

Comme en'écllair, i print l'pokeur qu'était tout rouge et i le traflli sus les jouonts d'chutte moin-là.

Quand la Sophie r'vint d'l'église et qu'a ouit les aventures de Charlie et son rouge pokeur, a s'en fut si sa vaisane pour li dire tout chi qui s'était arrivai durant l'temps qu'all'tait à l'église.

Savous bian qu'a trouvi sa vaisane bian embarrassai à env'loppai la moin de s'n haume!

Charlie heard some footsteps and he thought, "There's someone prowling about. I'm sure that it must be Germans." He was down in the hall and he saw a hand across the letter-box. It couldn't find the key because it wasn't there. Charlie had the presence of mind to put the poker in the fire.

Like lightning, he took the poker which was all red and he brought it down on the knuckles of that hand.

When Sophie came back from church and when she heard tell of Charlie's adventures and his red hot poker, she went to her neighbour's house to tell her all that had happened while she had been to church.

Do you know that she found her neighbour very busy wrapping up her husband's hand!

L'Olive et sa raonde dé papiers
par Gerald O Robilliard

L'onnaie 1920 lé *Guernsey Star* était imprimaï tard dans l'jour. Il
était delivraï à Torteva à quatre haeures l'arlevaïe, qui fait il était
niet l'hivaer quànd la paure Olive delivrait les papiers d'nouvelles
par les maisaons. Quand a passit l'église et l'chaemtière de Torteva,
a ouit des vouaix qui sortaient du chaemtière. I disaient
incessànment, "Ieun pour té et ieun pour mé, et daeux pour mé et
daeux pour té,"et a pensit, "I saont a charaïr les morts!"

All avait quatre soeurs qu'avaient mouru d'la consuptiaon.
Daeux d'iaeux avaient étai hardi bouannes mais les daeux aoutes
avaient étai désalaïe mauvaisès. Quànd a les ouit dire "Daeux pour
té et daeux pour mé." à pensit, "Ch'est mes soeurs qui saont a
charaïr!". All'tait si gênaie qu'all'tait comme aen lopin d'gllache.
Sa perchôine maisaon à delivraïr les journiaux ch'tait à la Grand'
Maison. Quand la Mary la vit à dit, "Sécours d'la vie, tchique t'as
Olive?"

S'fait l'Olive, " J'mé trouve pas bian. En passànt le chaemtiere
j'les ait ouit à charaïr les morts. P'tête qué ch'tait mes soeurs
qu'ils'taient à charïir."

La Mary lá print en d'dans et l'assievit dans enne grànd' chaire
mais la paure Olive avait riocque la maene d'la mort. All tait à la
monti hors dé counnisance. La Mary li dounnit du brandy et d'iauo
coaute. William sé trouvit dauve énne grosse putchie de castoignes.
Il avait étaï dauve lé vaisin Thoumas; ils avaient eputchis les
castoignes dans l'gardin du Probytère et avaient traversaïr la route,
et ils avaient charaï les castoignes sur l'tambe dans l'chaemtière
L'Olive ouvrisit ses iaers et dit, "Mes soeurs n'ànt pas l'naon
"castoigne", chest Ballogne comme mai Olive Ballogne."

Olive and her paper-round
by G O Robilliard

In the year 1920, the *Guernsey Star* was printed late in the day. It was delivered in Torteval at four o'clock in the afternoon, so it was dark in the winter when poor Olive delivered the newspapers round the houses. When she passed Torteval church and cemetery she heard some voices which came from the cemetery. She stopped and listened and she began to tremble from head to foot. They said incessantly, "One for you and one for me, and two for me and two for you," and she thought, "They're sharing out the dead!"

She had four sisters who had died from consumption. Two of them had been very good, but the other two had been really bad. When she heard them say two for you and two for me, she thought, "They are sharing out my sisters!" She was so frightened that she was like a lump of ice. The next house where she had to deliver the papers was "La Grand'Maison." When Mary saw her she said, "Good gracious, what's the matter Olive?"

Said Olive, "I don't feel very well. Whilst passing the cemetery, I heard them sharing out the dead. Perhaps it was my sisters they were sharing!"

Mary took her inside and sat her down in an armchair, but poor Olive just looked like death. She was half-fainting. Mary gave her some brandy and hot water. William arrived with a large bag full of chestnuts. He had been with his neighbour Thomas; they had picked up the chestnuts in the garden of the Rectory, had crossed the road and they had shared out the chestnuts on the tomb in the churchyard. Olive opened her eyes and said, "My sisters are not called Castoigne (chestnut), it's Ballogne like me, Olive Ballogne!"

La rougeur c'menchi à v'ni dans ses jaoes et quànd à vint à ses sens William y'expllitchi tchi qui s'était arrivaï. Mais ch'tait pas aen p'tit brandy qu'all'avait iaeut ch'en'tait aen fichu grand. A d'visait et riait comme enne fou. La v'là à continaïr sa route a delivraï les papiers. A chantait à haute vouaix:

Show me the way to go home,
I'm tired and I want to go to bed.
I had a little drink about an hour ago.
And it's gone right to my head.

Par lé temps qu'all'avait fini sa raonde dé papiers à marchait comme enne piratte. Ah la paure Olive. Nous a l'r'gret d'la paure Olive.

The colour started to come back to her cheeks, and when she came to her senses William explained what had happened to her. But it wasn't a small brandy that she had, it was a very big one. She talked and laughed like a mad thing. So off she went on her way to deliver the papers. She sang at the top of her voice:

> Show me the way to go home,
> I'm tired and I want to go to bed.
> I had a little drink about an hour ago,
> And it's gone right to my head.

By the time she had finished her paper-round, she walked like a duck. Ah poor Olive! We are sorry for poor Olive.

43

Le boudlo
par Terry Snell

Le chinq d'Novembe appeurchait et l's éfànts du fermier L'Sueur décidirent d'aver aën faëu pour brulaïr leaux boudlo sus l'haut d'la hougue.

Pour des jours, les éfànts furent embarrassaïr à trachier et tchériaer du bouais, du geon et d'la fouaille et tout tchi qui pouvaient maette moin d'sus qui brulait. La vielle aitre qu'avait'tai pllôine était quasi cllergie, tout était parti pour faire aën fichu grand faëu! Chéna fini, i restait rioque le boudlo a fabricher et ch'est qu'ils aeurent du pllaisi a l'faire. Vous eraitte rit s'vous l'avait vaëux. Il avait des brais d'tixaette et aën corset d'oeuvre qu'était pertussai comme aën criblle et aën naër saucepan comme haut boxe sus l'haut d'la tête. Ils mirent dans la chaisse d'laeux p'tite soeur pasque all avait des gràands reues et a n's'rait pas difficile a poussair.

Ils'taient si orgillaeux d'laeux boudlo qu'ils n'avaient pas la patience d'arrêtaïr pour lé chinq d'Novembre et i s'en furent lé pourmenair d'vànt.

Ch'est qu'ils en ramassirent des sous! Et comme tous les gens disaient, "Mais quai magnifique boudlo!" et dauve les sous i furent a la ville et acattirent aën gros boxe dé fireworks.

Enfin lé gràand jour vint et ils 'taient si excitai qué d'vànt n'aver iaeux laèux déjeunair ils s'en furent couorànt a la tchèrterie pour veies l'boudlo. Mais en aeurent ils aën choque quànd ils ouvrirent l'us. I parait qu'laëux gros naër tchen avait iaeux du pllaisi durànt la gniet! Ils trouvirent lé paoure boudlo en mille morciaux. Il avait perdu sa tête et ch'tait papier et hardes partout.

👈

The guy
by Terry Snell

The fifth of November was approaching and farmer Le Sueur's children decided to have a bonfire to burn their guy on top of the knoll.

For days the children were busy looking for and carrying wood, gorse and bracken and everything that they could find which burned. The old cow-shed which had been full was almost cleared; all was gone to make an extremely big bonfire. That finished, they only had to make the guy and they really had some fun making it. You would have laughed if you had seen it. He had corduroy trousers and an old guernsey which was full of holes like a sieve and he had a black saucepan like a top-hat on the top of his head. They put him in their little sister's pram because it had big wheels and it wouldn't be difficult to push.

They were so proud of their guy that they didn't have the patience to wait for the fifth of November and they took it out before that.

Well, they collected some money! As everybody said, "What a magnificent guy!" and with all the money they went to town and bought a big box of fireworks

At last the great day came and they were so excited that before having had their breakfast, they went running to the cart-shed to see the guy. But didn't they have a shock when they opened the door. It seems that their big black dog had had some fun during the night! They found the poor guy in a thousand pieces. He had lost his head and it was paper and clothes everywhere.

Mais y'en aeut du tinet! Ils plleurirent et heurlirent tànt qu'laeux père laeux dit, "N'vous genai pas, j'en érait enn'âoute près pour quànd vous viandratte dé l'école." Lé temps a l'école n'allait pas vite, mais a la fin v'la la clloque qui saonne et quànd i virrent a la maisaon a quatre haeures, i trouvirent aën gros boudlo dans la chaisse pret pour s'n allaïr par les maisaons. Mais ils'taient excitai! Ch'est qu'ils paraissait bian mux qué lé prumier, autcheuns n'eraient pas pus bael.

Dans bian p'tit d'temps ils'taient partis. Mais qu'ils allaient bian! Et bian vite laeux tin était quasi plloin. En arrivànt en haut du Campere, ils décidirent dé caomptair les sous pour aver aën p'tit r'las, et ch'est qu'y en avait!

Mais oye-ous! Dans l'excitement, ils raombillirent dé souognier à la chaisse, et quànd ils r'gardirent la chaisse était quasi au bas d'la rue et ch'est qu'al allait vite! Ch'tait comme enn éclair! Le boudlo était quâsi hors d'la chaisse et ses bras et djeret volaient partout.

A la fin, v'la chaisse et boudlo qui volirent frànc par d'sus l'fossai et finissirent lé faonds en haut dans l'prai au d'sous. Bian éffrai pasqué laeux mère les avait gernie dé grimair pas la chaisse, les éfants couorirent souvente.

Mais ils'taient chotchi quand ils vinrent au prai. Lé boudlo était a genouaies à s'coeurvair d'rire. Mais ils furent acore pus traompai quànd ils hallirent sen faux-visage, pasqué sav-ous, ch'tait daonc laeux père!

Well, there was some fuss! They cried and they howled so much that their father said to them, "Don't you worry, I will have another one ready for you when you come in from school." The time in school didn't go too quickly, but at last the bell rang and when they came home at four o'clock, they found a big guy in the pram ready to go round the houses. They were really excited! It really looked much better than the first , no-one would have a finer one.

In a very short time they were gone. Didn't they do well! Very soon their tin was almost full. On arriving at the top of Le Campère they decided to count the money to have a little respite, and there was a lot of it!

Well! In their excitement, they forgot to look after the pram, and when they looked, the pram was almost at the bottom of the road and wasn't it going fast! It was like lightning! The guy was almost out of the pram and his arms and legs were flying everywhere.

Finally the pram and the guy flew right over the hedge and finished upside down in the meadow below. Really frightened because their mother had warned them not to scratch the pram, the children ran after it.

Well, they were shocked when they came to the meadow. The guy was on his knees splitting his sides with laughter. They were even more amazed when they took off his mask, because, do you know what, it was their father!

Digniet
par Madeleine Squires-Beausire

Durànt la gniet quand lé maonde est endormi, les cahouans sant à trachier leur soupaï. Les crabbes sant embarrassaïes à faire leurs irognies. Les caoud-d'souoris volent raide bas et les pourchets d'fossai sant à s' pourménair. Les gens saont à dormir mais les haommes saont à raonfllaïr à évillier leurs faummes et leurs p'tits éfànts.

Lé p'tit Henri n'oimait pas la gniet, mais s'il avait énne p'tite làmpe allumaïe y'avait des aombres dans sa chàmbre. La grànde tchaire sembllait a énne grànde bête jutchie dans l'couogn, chèna lé faisait gerlottaïr, comme chèna il ôimrait mux n'aver pas d'vaeux au tout.

Quànd il faisait fin d'leune lé p'tit Henri gardait ses iaers bian cllos, mais il sembllait qu'i pouvait acore veies, Quànd il épiait y'avait les nuages qui travaersaient la leune et les brànques de l'arbre déhors sa f'nête sembllaient à des bras étendus prêts pour li. Il avait gardaï des chents coups à la leune mais il n'avait pas jomais vaeux lé viaer là–haout.

Opres aen p'tit temps il quaït endormi, et la catte du perchôin hu c'menchit à heurlaïr, "Miaow, Miaooow", Henri s'évillit raide éffraï, sautit du lliet et slippit d'sus la teile passequ'il avait latchi ses cauches au lliet. Sa sœur, la Rosie, lé ouit et s'l'vit à veies tchi il 'tait à faire, il plleurait et trembllait d'la tête es pids et a' l'embrachit et le r'mit au lliet.

Rosie li dit énne p'tite histouaire pour l'aidger à dormir, a' li dit que les ànges au ciel gardaient sur li et il fallaït pas ête éffraï. Rosie lé baisit et dit, "Que Lé bouan Dju té bénie."

Night-time
by Madeleine Squires-Beausire

During the night when the world is asleep, the owls are seeking their supper. The spiders are busy spinning their webs. The bats swoop low and the hedgehogs are about. Folk are asleep but the men are snoring fit to wake their wives and children.

Little Henry did not like night time, but if he had a little lamp lit there were shadows in his bedroom. The big chair looked like a big animal, crouching in the corner, that made him tremble, like that he would prefer not to have a light at all.

When it was moonlight little Henry kept his eyes tightly closed, but it seemed that he could still see. When he peeped out there were clouds passing across the moon and the branches of the tree outside his window seemed like arms stretching out ready to grab him. He had looked at the moon hundreds of times but he had never seen the old man up there.

After a little while he fell asleep, and the cat from next door began to cry, "Miaow, Miaoow", Henry woke up scared stiff, jumped out of bed and slipped on the lino because he had left his socks on in bed. His sister, Rosie, heard him and got up to see what he was doing, he was crying and trembling from head to foot and she took him in her arms and put him back to bed.

Rosie told him a little story to help him to sleep, she told him that the angels in Heaven were watching over him and that he must not be afraid. Rosie kissed him and said, "May God bless you."

En Mair
par Madeleine Squires-Beausire

Aen jour duràant l'étaï lé William et la Cécile décidirent d'allaïr autour de Guernési dans leur baté, il 'tait seize pids laong, pouôinturaï aen biau bllu dauve des manifiques rouges vêles. Le ciel était bllu dauve énne tràntchille brise, comme chèna il pouvaient lé maette à la vêle, mais il avaient aen p'tit engin en cas qu'y avait pas d'vent.

Ils sortizirent de Saint Pierre Port au matin et furent enviaers lé nord pour Saint Samsaon, pâssirent le Havre de Bordeaux, à travaers lé pâssage en d'dans d'la Platte Fougère et puis firent lé tour pour L'Ancresse. La Cécile dit que l'île paraissait différente d'la maïr et la bànque ne paraissait pas si grànde comme à terre.

Ils continuirent pour Grand Havre, mais y avait énn amas d' rotchets et la Cécile s'assiévit dans lé naïz du baté pour guettaïr. Y avait des temps qu'a pouvait quâsi touchier les rotchets et veies jusque des fllies. I' pouvaient veies l'éghise du Vale et le châté et l'éghise du Câtel, et pis i' furent pour Cobo. Ch'tait intêressant de veies ouecque les gens d'meuraient qu'ils counnissaient, et chéna aidgait à passaïr lé temps.

Oprès ils pâssirent le Vazon pour la Perelle. La Cécile c'menchait à aver fôim et sé, mais dans aen baté (comme énne grànde flotte) il fallait pas bère trop, et pis i' firent lé tour de Lihou à travaers la bànque de Rocquôine, le vent tout d'aen caoup empllit les vêles et le baté volit pour le Portelet. Il ancrirent là pour mangier leurs doraies. Le soleil avait disparu et il 'tait temps d'allaïr pour le pouôint de Pleinmont, le laong d'la caoute du sud. Quand ils pâssirent Le Long Cavaleux, le William dit qué ch'tait énne bouane piaeche pour allaïr à basse iaoue pour des gros ormés.

On the Sea
by Madeleine Squires-Beausire

One day during the summer William and Cécile decided to go around Guernsey in their boat, it was sixteen feet long, painted blue with magnificent red sails. The sky was blue with a light breeze, so they could set the sail, but they had a little motor in case there was no wind.

They sailed out of St. Peter Port in the morning and went towards the north for St. Sampson's, past Bordeaux harbour through the passage inside the Platte Fougère then round for l'Ancresse. Cécile said that the island looked different from the sea and the beach did not look as big as from land.

They went on towards Grand Havre, but there were a lot of rocks and Cécile went and sat in the bow to keep watch. There were times when she could almost touch them and even see the limpets. They could see the Vale church and the castle and Câtel church and then on to Cobo. It was interesting to see where people they knew lived, and that helped to pass the time.

Afterwards they passed Vazon on the way to Perelle. Cécile was beginning to get hungry and thirsty but in a boat (like a big open boat) one must not drink too much, and then around Lihou across Rocquaine bay, suddenly the wind filled the sails and the boat flew on towards Portelet. They anchored there to eat their sandwiches. The sun had disappeared and it was time to make for Pleinmont point, along the south coast. When they passed the Long Cavaleux, William said that it was a good place to go at low water to get big ormers.

Ils pâssïrent P'tit Bot pour Saint Martin et la maïr c'menchit à remoutcher et il faisait fré et la Cécile voulait maette ses chiraïs, mais coum-tchi? A'n'pouvait pas même se gardaïr d'but ou all' érait paie tcheies hors-rabord. Le William dévirit le baté et il arrêtit. A la pouôinte de Saint Martin la maïr c'menchit a p'tit à roulaïr dans les couorànts et la Cécile avait énne grànde envie d'êt'e à la maisaon. A' s'assiévit en d'vant du William et aen souel vint pardessus le gonnel et avau son co et a' fut trempaïe. Le William était saec et tournit sa tête passequ'il voulait rire. La Cécile dounnit aen grànd soupir, a' pouvait veies Châté Cornet et la maïr était bian tràntchille pour prende le baté en saeurtaï pour Saint Pierre Port.

They passed P'tit Bôt for St. Martin's and the sea began to get rough and it was cold and Cécile wanted to put on her oilskins, but how? She could not even stand up or she could have been thrown overboard. William altered course and the boat stopped. At St. Martin's point the sea began to roll a bit with the currents and Cécile really longed to be back home. She sat down in front of William and a swell came over the side and down her neck and she was soaked. William was dry and turned his head away because he wanted to laugh. Cécile heaved a great sigh she could see Castle Cornet and the sea was nice and calm to take the boat safely to St. Peter Port.

Le Lundi
par Madeleine Squires - Beausire

Au lundi matin il fallait allumaïr lé faeu sous lé coppeur et pis paompaïr iaoue dé dans la faountôine et tchériaïr des bouquetaies iaoue pour empllir lé coppeur pour faire lé lavïn. (L'hivaer il l'avait des verraennes jusque au but du naiz). Quànd iaoue était caoud assaiz il fallait halair iaoue dauve a boutchet et pis versair dans a baillot pour lé r'empllir, pour maette lé linge à trempaïr dauve du savaon 'Marsielle', (il fallait pas est à la môinti au dormir à faire chen'chin, il érait paeu est brûlaï.)

Opres il fallait rôinchier à iaoue caoud et pis à iaoue frêde dauve du 'Blue', pour lé bllanc linge et pis turtre lé linge à la môin. (Et y'avais d'la pôine dauve les deigts pllione d'refredaeure et les boutchets qui v'nir raide b'sant à la veis qui l'alles.)

Il fallait étende déhors sur les cords à linge et quand ils etaient pllôin il fallait maette lé restant sur du jaon, mais si y'avais des tacs il fallait maette lé linge su l'herbe tout la gniet à la roussaïe.

Aen caoup sec il fallait qui ce férraïr, il fallait enne pllanche de bouais couvair dauve a bllantchet et a lincheur pour ferraïr d'su la table et en pllatoine dé faer pour maette lé faer à férraïr d'sus. Il mettait daeux faers à cauffair sur lé raenge ou dans l'atre et épis il faillait épllutcher a faer dauve en empouogn et dans l'aute môin enne grosses chiques pour lé torchier pour si y'avais des fllamêques. Y'avais étout à emp'sair les doubillers, les entchaeures, les bllànc sertouts et les colets qu'minse.

Au saer y'avais à ramendaïr et coude des boutaons dauve la vaeux de la làmpe a parafaenne.

On Mondays
by Madeleine Squires-Beausire

On Monday mornings we had to light the fire under the copper and then pump water from the well and carry buckets full of water to fill the copper to do the washing. (In winter there were icicles right on the end of one's nose). When the water was hot enough we had to ladle out the water with a bucket then pour it into a tub to fill it, to put the washing to soak with some Marseille soap, (you must not be half asleep when you were doing that or you could have been scalded).

Afterwards we had to rinse in hot water and then in cold with some "Blue" for the whites and then wring the washing by hand. (And it was hard with cold hands and the buckets becoming very heavy as they went along.)

We had to hang it out on washing lines and when they were full put the rest on the gorse, but if there were stains we had to put the washing on the grass all night in the dew.

Once it was dry it had to be ironed, we needed a wooden board covered with a blanket and an ironing sheet over the table and an iron stand to put the iron on. We put two irons to heat up on the range or in the hearth and then we had to pick up the iron with a holder and in the other hand we had a thick rag to wipe it in case there were smuts. Also we had to starch the table-cloths, the white aprons and the shirt collars.

In the evening we had to mend and sew on buttons by the light of an oil lamp.

Énne tchuriaeuse Pourménade
par Harry Tomlinson

Il avait fait si caoud toute la s'môine qué nous n'pouvait pas travaillier dans les spans après méjeu. Ch'tait comme les jours d'étaï d'enne achie, quànd nous était jône. Chu jour-là, i n'y avait pas d'nuages dans le ciel et la terre était cratchie parce qu'all'tait si saec. Vers six haeures et d'mie je m'avisis dé faire enne p'tite pourmenade et d'allaïr veir combian d'iaoue qu'i y avait dans le reservoir. Je prins mon chapé, je criyis pour le tchian et nous v'là partis.

Après la chaleur de l'arlevaïe i c'menchait à amolir aën p'tit, et parmi les arbres, près du reservoir nous était pus caonfortablle. Le tchian était haeuraeux à trachier des p'tites bêtes dans l'herbe, et mé, je marchais lentement sans pensaïr à grand chaose. Tout était tràntchille, nous n'pouvait ouïr rian – pas énne créature n'bougeait. J'étais aën p'tit ravi de veir qué l'iaoue était si haute après tànt de jours sans pllie. Tout d'aën caoup, au llian, l'hologe d'l'égllise de St. Sauveur c'menchit à sounnaïr sept haeures.

Je r'gardis l'iaoue. All'tait compllétement pllate, comme aën miraeux, ou putaot comme enn'ozaune, passequ'i mé resembllait qué je pouvais veir à travaers, frànc au faond. Et, là-bas, au faond, tout était cllaïre comme le jour.

Je creyais qué je pouvais veir tchiques bâtiments. I y avait enne grànde maisaon dauve aën p'tit gardin d'vànt. I' n'y avait pas de flleurs, mais i y avait d'l'herbe ouéqu'i'y avait daeux tablles et chinq ou six tchaires. Toutes les f'nêtres étaient ouvaertes, et l'hus de d'vànt étout. Daeux vieux haommes, étaient assis au soleil, sus aën banc, d'vànt ieune des f'nêtres. Il avaient laeux p'tits corsets déboutonnaïs et laeux chapiaux poussaïs en arrière.

A Strange Walk
by Harry Tomlinson

The weather had been so hot all week that we could not work in the greenhouses after mid-day. It was like the hot summer days of times gone by, when we were young. That day there wasn't a cloud in the sky and the ground was cracked because it was so dry. Towards half past six I decided to go for a walk and go and see how much water there was in the reservoir. I took my hat, and called the dog and off we went.

After the heat of the afternoon it was beginning to grow a bit cooler, and amidst the trees, by the reservoir we were more comfortable. The dog was happy to look for little creatures in the grass, and I walked along slowly without thinking of anything in particular. Everything was peaceful, and you could not hear a sound – not a thing stirred. I was a bit surprised to see that the water was so high after so many days without rain. All of a sudden, in the distance, the clock of St. Saviour's church began to strike seven.

I looked at the water. It was completely flat, like a mirror, or rather like a pane of glass, because it seemed to me that I could see through it, right to the bottom. And there, at the bottom, everything was as bright as day.

I thought I could see some buildings. There was a big house with a little garden in front of it. There were no flowers, but there was grass where there were two tables and five or six chairs. All the windows were open, and the front door as well. Two old men were sitting in the sun on a bench in front of one of the windows. They had their waistcoats unbuttoned and their hats pushed back.

Ente les daeux têtes je pouvais veir le visage d'énn aoute haoume qui laeux d'visait de d'dans. Je n'saïs pas chu qu'i disait mais de temps en temps i s'bouffirent à rire.

Dans la rue aën ch'va était amarraï à aën rang dans la muraille. Il avait ses âtelles acore et tout le temps sa queue bougeait, et i tapait ses sabots sus le pavaï. Sans doute, les mouques le pitchaient et ne li dounnaient pas dé r'paos.

Par terre, sous enn'arbre, i y avait daeux fourques à foin, aën râté et aën chapé d'paille.

Treis gaillards étaient assis à ieune des tables dauve des mogues à cidre et enne djougue. Tout d'aën caoup enne jône fille dauve aën bllanc d'vànté sortisit d'l'hus. A portait treis assiaettes et a vint les maette sus la tablle. I me resembllait qué le sent du r'vasi, – du jambaon et des oues fricachis – vint frànc à mon naïz!

Comme i c'menchaient à mangier, ieun des jônes haommes li dit tchique chaose. La démouaiselle sourit, et li dounnit énne répaonse, en ritounnànt, et les daeux aoutes s'mirent à rire comme des perdus. À chu moment-là, aën famaeux haomme s'mourtit à l'hus. Il avait les mànches de sa qu'minse r'leuvaïes et aën torchaon à vessiaoux comme aën seratout. Sans doute ch'tait le patron, - et pis je r'mertchis enne pllanche au dessus d'l'hus. Je manigis de déchiffraïr les mots pouôinturaïs déssus, "Royal Oak, J. Alexandre". Ch'tait le cabaret sus la Neuve Rue, qui fut couvaert par l'iaoue quànd i firent le reservoir.

Le cabartcher r'gardit le ciel, pis i dit tchique chaose ès jônes haoumes, qui l'virent laeux mogues vers li, en monière de santaïe. D'vant de disparaitre i marmounnit aën mot à la fille, qui ramassit la djougue et s'en fut vite vers l'hus.

Bian que je fusse llian du bâtiment, i me r'sembllait que je pouvais ouïr des vouaix rounnaïr dans le cabaret, et en des temps des gens qui riaient. Je pouvais sentir la fumaïe dé touba, et pis tchiqu'un c'menchit à sounnaïr aën violaon ou enne chifournie. Bietaot je pouvais ouïr la chànt'rie, et des bottes à sparabilles, qui tappaient sus le pllànchet.

156

Between the two heads I could see the face of another man who was speaking to them from inside. I don't know what he was saying, but from time to time they burst out laughing.

In the lane a horse was tied to a ring in the wall. He still had his harness on and all the time his tail swished, and he stamped his hooves on the cobbles. No doubt the flies were biting him and giving him no peace.

On the ground, under a tree, there were two pitchforks, a rake and a straw hat.

Three young men were sitting at one of the tables with cider mugs and a stoneware jug. Suddenly a young girl with a white apron came out of the door. She was carrying three plates and she came a put them on the table. It seemed that the delicious smell – of fried ham and eggs – came right to my nostrils!

As they started to eat, one of the young men said something to her. The young girl smiled, and answered him back with a giggle, and the two others fell about with laughter. At that moment a large man appeared in the doorway. He had his shirtsleeves rolled up and a tea towel as an apron. No doubt he was the landlord, and then I noticed a board above the door. I managed to make out the words painted on it, "Royal Oak, J. Alexandre". It was the inn on the Neuve Rue, which was covered by the water when they made the reservoir.

The innkeeper looked at the sky, then he said something to the young men, who raised their mugs in his direction in the way of a toast. Before disappearing he muttered something to the young girl, who picked up the jug and hurried off towards the door.

Although I was a long way from the building, it seemed that I could hear the sound of voices in the inn, and from time to time people laughing. I could smell tobacco smoke, and then someone started to play a violin or a hurdy gurdy. Soon I could hear singing and hobnailed boots tapping on the floor.

Tout d'aën caoup, aën tchian sortisit et c'menchit à bractaïr. Le ch'va, amarraï à la muraille, l'vit sa tête et baillit aën cri. I r'chut énne répaonse à l'haeure, et pis je vis qu'a v'nait d'enn aoute ch'va qui d'valait la rue dauve aën laong tchériot. I marchait douochement. Aën viaer haomme le m'nait par le brideau et y avait enne vieille faumme de l'aoute cotaï du ch'va. A t'nait aën ponier et enne grande caune-à-lait, et all'avait son d'vànté et aën chapé d'paille.

Sus le daos du ch'va y avait enne fille d'à peu près dix-sept ans. A t'nait la sélette d'ieune de ses môins et d'l'aoute môin a t'nait son scoop qu'all'avait halaï. Aën jône haomme marchait à cotaï d'ielle dauve sa môin sus son genouaï, p'tête pour l'empêchier de tcheir, ou p'tête passequ'alle avait de belles gambes!

Tout chu qu'i y avait dans le tchériot étaient daeux filles, jutchies caote à caote sus le bord, et daeux jônes haommes d'but, appllaïs caonte les écouars. Quànd le tchériot s'arrêtit les quatre sautirent bas, et l'aoute jône haomme aidgit la sianne sus le ch'va à d'valaïr. Il entrirent dans le p'tit "gardin" éiouque les aoutes étaient à mangier, et il échàngirent tchiques mots. Ieune des filles éputchit aën p'tit morsé de jambaon et le fourit dans sa bouche, et s'n amie print ieun des mogues de déssus la tablle et avalit enne grànde gorgie. Les haommes à la tablle firent la maene d'ête gueurvaïs, tandis que les aoutes cueurvaient dé rire.

Le patron apparut dans huss'rie pour veir chu qui s'arrivait, mais quànd i vit qué ch'tait rioque la jouerie, i chaquit sa tête et sourit. Pis i vit le vaier haomme qui m'nait le ch'va et i li cryit tchique chaose. Je creis que je l'ouis d'mandaïr "le drôin viage?" -et la répaonse. "Oué, ch'est tout fini, Dju merci." Il échàngirent acore tchiques mots, pis le viaer hâlit sus le brideau et le ch'va erc'menchit à marchier.

All of a sudden, a dog came out and started to bark. The horse tied up to the wall, lifted his head and let out a whinny. He received an answer immediately, and then I saw that it came from another horse coming down the road with a long hay cart. He was walking slowly. An old man was leading him by the bridle and there was an old woman on the other side of the horse. She was carrying a basket a large milk "can", and she was wearing an apron and a straw hat.

On the horse's back was a girl of about seventeen years old. She was holding on to the harness with one hand and in the other hand she was holding her scoop bonnet which she had taken off. A young man was walking alongside her with his hand on her knee, perhaps to stop her from falling off, or perhaps because she had nice legs!

All there was in the cart were two girls perched side by side on the edge, and two young men standing , leaning against the back poles. When the cart stopped, the four of them jumped off, and the other young man helped the girl on the horse to get down. They went into the little "garden" where the others were eating, and exchanged a few words. One of the girls pinched a bit of ham and popped it into her mouth and her friend grabbed one of the mugs from the table and drank a great mouthful. The men at the table pretended to be angry, whilst the others fell about with laughter.

The landlord appeared in the doorway to see what was going on, but when he saw that it was nothing but skylarking, he shook his head and smiled. Then he saw the old man who was leading the horse and he shouted something to him. I thought I heard him asking "the last load?" and the answer. "Yes, it's all finished, thank goodness." They exchanged a few more words, then the old man pulled on the bridle and the horse walked on.

Il écanchit qué l'haomme tournit son visage dans ma direction. Il 'tait bian llian, mais quànd je r'gardis, i me risembllait qué je le counissais! Je me sentais aën p'tit éffraï, car j'étais saeur qué ch'tait l'haomme dans la picture qui soulait ête sus le mur dans le parlaeux dé mes grandparents, quànd j'étais p'tit! Ch'tait enne picture d'laeux ferme ès Annevilles. Ch'tait le temps du fôin, et y avait la maisaon, les tas d'foin, les ch'vaux et les tchériots et toute la fomille.

I r'gardit vers mé pour tchiques ségaonds, pis i tournit sa tête et dit tchique chaose à sa faumme, et i cantinuirent sus laeux ch'min.

Au mesme instànt daeux piraettes volirent au déssus de ma tête et d'valirent sus l'iaoue. Le "verre" fut buchi en mille morciaux et le cabaret, le tchériot et les gens – tous disparurent à l'haeure.

Je r'gardis autouor d'mé. Les mouissaons étaient à chàntaïr derchies, et je pouvais ouir le camas d'aën tracteur dans le courti derrière mé. Mon tchian était à mes pids, prêt à cantinuaïr not'e pourmenade, et tout était comme de couteume. Mais, mé, je tâchais dé caomprendre chu qui s'était arrivaï. Je me d'màndis, "Était-che aën saonge? Combian de temps avais-je passaï à r'gardaïr chutte scène? Dix minutes? Enne demie haeure?" – Je ne savais pas. Pis j'ouis l'hologe de l'égllise de St. Sauveur. I n'avait pas acore fini de sounnaïr sept haeures! Qui fait, tout chena s'était passaï dans aën cllin d'iel! Les gens qué j'avais vaeus pour aën ségaond durànt ma tchuriaeuse pourmenade, étaient – i mes grandparents – ou des r'vénànts?

The man happened to turn his face in my direction. He was a long way off, but when I looked, it seemed to me that I knew him! I felt a bit scared, for I was sure that it was the man in the picture which used to be on the wall in my grandparents' parlour, when I was little! It was a picture of their farm at Les Annevilles. It was haymaking time, and there was the farm house, the haystacks, the horses and carts and all the family.

He looked towards me for a few seconds, then he turned his head and said something to his wife, and they continued on their way.

At the same moment two ducks flew over my head and came down onto the water. The "glass" was shattered into a thousand pieces and the inn, the cart and the people – all disappeared immediately.

I looked around me. The birds were singing again, and I could hear the sound of a tractor in the field behind me. My dog was at my feet ready to continue our walk and everything was as usual. But I tried to understand what had happened. I asked myself, "Was it a dream? How long had I spent watching this scene? Ten minutes? Half an hour?" – I didn't know. Then I heard the sound of St. Saviour's church. It hadn't yet finished striking seven o'clock! So all that had happened in the blink of an eye! The people I had seen for a second during my strange walk – were they my grandparents – or ghosts?

La Chivière
par Harry Tomlinson

Ma vieille chivière, quaï triste spectaclle que tu fais auch't'haeure, là-bas au couogn d'la tchérterie, quasi muchie sous aen tas de câsses et de baenques. Le bouais de tes fllancs est tout usaï et tes bras saont tous fendus. Hélas, t'as portaï ton drôin viâge, ta vie est finie, tu n'es pus bouan à rien. Veis-tu, j'ai apportaï ma hache, et dans tchiques minutes nous t'era en morciaux. Mais, tu pourras me faire aen drôin service, ton bouais pourra allumaïr mon faeu et cauffaïr ma maisaon aen p'ti. Arrête que j'allume ma pipe.

Je m'en r'souviens, ch'tait l'onclle Alfrat qui te fit, le frère de mon père. Ch'tait aen bouan tcherpentcher, li. I'savait bien son métier. Je peux le veir acore dans sa tcherpenterie, dauve sa grosse calotte, en manches dè c'minse, d'but d'vant s'n établlie, parmi ses outils, tous bian aidguchis. Il 'tait p'tit, dauve des raondes lunaettes, et quaend le soleil les tapaient nous ne pouvait pas veir ses bllus iers. Ses môins étaient grosses et rendurcies d'aveir t'nu la scie et le marté durant des onnaïes. Mais ses gros deigts strôtchaient le bouais comme ch'tait la pieau d'aen éfànt et quand i' poussait son rabot les dôlaeures suffllaient et volaient comme des ribans de souaie, et la médale sus la chôine de sa maonte châtchait et tappait caontre son p'tit corset.

Quaend i' t'aumnit ciz naon il 'tait bian fiar de son travas, car, dauve ta neuve bllue pointure t'étais belle comme enne jonne fille graïe pour les neuches. Vraiment, t'étais trop belle pour allaïr travaillier dans les spans et les courtils. L'onclle Alfrat t'avait fait dauve le mesme souogn et patienche que s'il fachounnait aen cabinet ou enne tabllle pour le parlair. Il 'tait terjous comme chéna quaend i' travaillait! I' disait, "I' faut mesuraïr daeux caoups et copaïr riocqu' aen caoup!"

The Wheelbarrow
by Harry Tomlinson

My old wheelbarrow, what a sorry sight you make now, there in the corner of the shed, half hidden under a pile of boxes and baskets. Your wooden sides are all worn away and your handles are split. Alas, you have carried your last load, your life is over, you're no longer any use for anything. Do you see, I've brought my axe, and in a few minutes we'll have you in pieces. But you can do me one last service, your wood can light my fire and warm my house a bit. Wait 'til I light my pipe.

I recall, it was uncle Alfred who made you, my father's brother. Now he was a good carpenter. He really knew his trade. I can see him now in his workshop, with his big cap, in his shirt sleeves, standing at his bench amongst his tools, all beautifully sharpened. He was little, with round spectacles, and when the sun hit them we couldn't see his blue eyes. His hands were big and hardened from years of holding a saw and a hammer. But his big fingers stroked the wood as if it were a child's skin, and when he used his plane the shavings whistled and flew like silken ribbons, and the medallion on his watch chain swung and tapped against his waistcoat.

When he brought you to our house he was really pleased with his work, for, with your new blue paint, you were as beautiful as a young girl dressed up for a wedding. Really, you were too beautiful to go and work in the greenhouses and the fields. Uncle Alfred had made you with the same care and patience as if he were creating a cabinet or a table for the parlour. He was always like that when he worked! He used to say, "You must measure twice and only cut once!"

☛

Dans tes premiers jours nous te faisait servir duouchement et t'étais comme la nouvelle mariaïe qu'apprend les couteumes et les monières de sa nouvelle fomille, mais bétaot tu prins ta pieache dans not'e maonde. Tu passais des journaïes dans les spans et tu sentais la sueur et la fumaïe de toubac des haommes qui faisaient les trenchies, courbais sus laeux beques. És autes jours t'étais sous les vaegnes dauve les faummes et t'écoutais laeux jass'rie parmi les fielles et la grappe. Bêque et raté, sertchaeux et cisiaux, tous les outils, tu les counnissais, et tu les portais et rapportais matin et saer. Tu portais toutes sortes de cartchaisaons, et i'n'fallait pas ête trop chafernaeuse nitout, parce que t'étais oblligie de portaïr des viâges de cour pour engraissier la terre et de tcherbaon pour cauffaïr les spans et pour la stimm'rie.

Ah, t' r'souviens-tu d'la stimm'rie? – ches gniéties que nous passait dans le sent de la fumaïe et d'la terre caoude. Ch'tait dur chu travas-là. Nous allait et r'v'nait ente le boileur et le span, enne minute trempaï de sueur, pis g'laï par le vent d'hivaer. Combien de caoups, vers les treis haeures, m'sis-ju assis ente tes bras, tout épuisaï, pour hautaïr aen p'ti, d'vant dé r'c'menchier.

Et pis y avait les matinaïes à tchillier les "daffs" dans les courtils, dauve la pael de nos deigts tout cratchie par le fré et irritaïe par le sève des flleurs.

Ah, j'n'oïmais pas les jours d'hivaer, saouf quaend nous avait enne haeure ou daeux de libre pour allaïr à la basse iaoux. Dans la banque, parmi les rocques, nous était trempaï et g'laï derchier, mais chu caoup nous n'l'sentait pas – ch'tait différent là-bas. Si nous avait not' croc dans la môin et nous avait trouvaï enne bouanne piaeche toute plloine d'ormés, nous r'mertchit pas la frédure perchànte du vent. Nous travaillait bian vite et dé bouan tchoeur pour n'ête pas battu par le montànt d'la maïr. Tu t'resouviens, sans doute, de chutte onnaïe quaend i'y avait tant d' ormés que je n'pouvais pas les portaïr mé mesme et je fus oblligi de v'nir te trouvaïr pour m'aïdger. Cor chapin, chu caoup-là, nous en avait des douzoines. I'y en avait assaïz pour tous les Pipiaux!

164

In your early days we used you gently, and you were like the newly wed who is learning the customs and ways of her new family, but soon you took your place in our world. You spent days in the greenhouses and you smelt the sweat and tobacco smoke of the men bent over their spades, digging the trenches. On other days you were under the vines with the womenfolk and you listened to their chatter amongst the leaves and the grapes. Spade and rake, weeder and scissors, you knew all the tools, and you carried them back and forth morning and evening. You carried all sorts of loads, and you hadn't to be too choosy either, because you had to carry loads of muck to manure the ground and coal to heat the greenhouses and for steaming.

Ah, do you remember steaming? – those nights which we spent in the smell of smoke and hot earth. It was hard, that work. We went backwards and forwards between the boiler and the greenhouse, one minute soaked with sweat, then chilled through by the winter wind. How many times, around three o'clock in the morning, did I sit down exhausted, to grab forty winks between your arms, before starting off again.

And then there were the mornings picking "daffs" in the fields, with the skin of our fingers all cracked by the cold and irritated by the sap from the flowers.

Oh, I didn't like the winter days, except when we had an hour or two free to go ormering. Down on the beach, amongst the rocks, we were soaked and frozen again, but this time we didn't feel it – it was different down there. If we had our hook in our hand and we had found a good place, full of ormers, we didn't notice the biting cold of the wind. We worked quickly and willingly, not to be beaten by the rising tide. You no doubt remember that year when there were so many ormers that I couldn't carry them and I had to come and fetch you to help me. Cor chapin, that time we had dozens of them. There were enough for all the Pipets!

Mes ouecqu'i' saont partis, les ormés? Ogniet nous n'en veit pas la couleur, certôinement pas assaïz pour aen bouan fricot!

Et pis i y avait les jours de tàmpête qu'apportaient le vraic et le capari. Nous en a ram'naï des chiv'raïes, té et mé! Nous était fichi à la fin d'la journaïe, et il fallait que je graississe bian ta reue pour empêchier le roule, mais le vraic était bouan pour la terre et le bouais pour le faeu – et i'n'coûtaient pas aen pénni!

Mais ch'tait les jours d'étaï que j'oïmais le mux, bian que nous fusse bian embarrassaï dauve les tamates et la grappe. Toute la journaïe nous était là dans les spans, parmi les haoutes pllàntes qui couleuraient de vaert nos môins et nos c'minses et y lâtchaient laeux tchuriaeux sent. Cor, faisait-i caoud là-d'dans, même quaend nous avait causaï le verre pour dounaïr aen p'ti d'aombre.

Souvent tu restais dans le shed dauve les faummes qu'étaient à sortaïr, à b'saïr et à patcher les tamates. Tu respirais le sent des frits et du bouais sciaï des "chips", prêts à ête empllis. Les p'tis caoups d'vent qu'entraient par l'us, large ouvaert, faisaient vol'taïr le fin papier, bllu, bllanc et couleur de rose.

Pour le mio-matin t'étais not' tablle. Nous te mettait à l'aombre sous les arbres pour t'ni le pot à thée, les coupes et les assiettaïes de galaettes ou de gâche. Nous sipotait not' thée douochement, et nous targiait sus la daeuxième coupaïe, pas trop preissi pour r'c'menchier. Les éfànts jouaient sus la chôlaette et quiquefeis, quaend "la tablle" était cllergie, i'v'naient te prendre pour laeux gaumes, et pour iaeux t'étais tchériot, môto, baté et je n'saïs tchi! Te r'mets-tu, enn an, i' te couvrirent de flleurs pour le "North Show"? Cor, étaient-i' fiaers le jour du chaoux, dans laeux costumes. Je n'saïs puis chu qu'il 'taient mais il avaient prins daeux journaïes pour te décoraïr, et nous tappit les môins comme des fous quaend nous te vit dans la parade. Tu ne gognis pas le prumier prix, ni le daeuxième nitout, mais les cragniaons étaient bian orguillaeux d'laeux certificat, et i'n'nous alouirent pas de halaïr tes flleurs d'vant qu'i'n'fussent toutes saecs et mortes!

But where have they gone, the ormers? Today we don't see a sign of them, certainly not enough for a good feed!

And then there were the stormy days which brought in the seaweed and the flotsam. We've brought back barrowloads, you and I. We were shattered at the end of the day and I had to give your wheel a good greasing to stop the rust, but the seaweed was good for the soil and the driftwood for the fire – and they didn't cost a penny!

But it was the summer days I liked best, even though we were busy with the tomatoes and grapes. All day long we were there in the greenhouses, amongst the tall plants which stained our hands and shirts green and left their strange smell on them. Cor, wasn't it hot in there, even when we had lime-washed the glass to give a bit of shade.

Often you stayed in the shed with the women who were grading, weighing and packing the tomatoes. You breathed in the smell of the fruit and the sawn wood of the "chips" waiting to be filled. The little gusts of wind which came in through the wide-open door caused the blue, white and pink tissue paper to flutter.

For "elevens" you were our table. We would put you in the shade under the trees to hold the tea pot, the cups and the plates of Guernsey biscuits or gâche. We sipped our tea slowly, and lingered over the second cupful, not in too much of a hurry to get back to work. The children played on the swing, and sometimes, when the "table" was cleared, they would come and take you for their games, and for them you were cart, motor car, boat and I don't know what else. Do you remember, one year, they covered you with flowers for the "North Show"? Cor, weren't they pleased on the day of the show, dressed in their costumes. I don't know what they were supposed to be, but they had taken two days to decorate you, and we clapped like mad when we saw you in the parade. You didn't win first prize, or even second, but the kids were very proud of their certificate, and they wouldn't allow us to take off your flowers until they were all dry and dead!

Quaend nous chàngit à l'huile pour cauffaïr les spans, la vie d'vint aen p'ti pus aisi pour nous daeux, nous n'tait pas d'aoute oblligi d'allaïr tchériaïr le tcherbaon et de stôtcher le boileur chaque saer. Mais bétaot le prix d'l'huile c'menchit à hauchier et le prix des tamates à d'valaïr. Les experts nous dirent de chàngier de récolte et nous c'menchit à creitre des flleurs. Te v'là, couvaerte d'flleurs derchier! À chu temps i'y avait des potaïes d'flleurs partout, supareillement juste d'vant "Mothering Sunday" quaend i' fallait travaillier gniet et jeur pour que les flleurs fussent au marchi pour les millaeurs prix

Mais les dépenses continuirent à maontaïr maugré tous nos éfforts. Nous pllàntit toutes sortes dé tché, des frits que nous n'avait jomais vaeus, des "kiwi fruit" et ches tchuriaeux "babaco". (Je n'saïs pas comme tchi que nous mange d'itaï tché!) Nous éprouvit tout.

Mais i faut qu' les temps changent!. Les éfànts ne voulaient pas travaillier dans les spans comme naon et les v'là partis pour trachier du travas dans la ville, - et quaend nous veit les sous qu'il y gognent, cor chapin, il aont bian fait! Mais, quaend-même, i' saont oblligis de s'l'vaïr et de partir du partemps, d'vant qu'i' fait jeur, pour l'amour d'la parc'erie. I mangent laeux déjunaï et i s'rasent dans le moto, car, s'il arrivent dans la ville trop tard i'n'y pas de piaeche!

Ichin, l'affaire est finie, comme tu veis – dauve mon rhoumatise, je ne pouvais pas caontinuaïr à trimaïr – et pouôinturaïr les spans- et le prix du – ah bah! v'là ma pipe étôinte!

Véyaons, tchique je m'en allais faire? Ah, oué, v'là ma hache, j'allais te défaoncaïr. Mais quand j'y pense, je n'pourrais pas te faire du mal. Nous a vieilli ensemblle, té et mé. T'es la cronique de ma vie! Ah, je cllergirai la crache enn aoute jour. Je te laisserai tràntchille dans ton couogn. Tu mérites bian ton r'paos. Adi, ma vieille amie. Si les vaers viennent te mangier, qu'i'l' fachent duouchement!

When we changed to oil for heating the greenhouses life became a bit easier for us both, we no longer had to go and get the coal and stoke the boiler every night. But soon the price of oil began to go up and the price of tomatoes to go down. The experts told us to change crops and we began to grow flowers. There you were, covered with flowers again! In those days there were jars of flowers everywhere, especially just before "Mothering Sunday" when we had to work night and day so that the flowers were at the market for the best prices.

But the costs continued to rise in spite of all our efforts. We planted all sorts of things, fruits which we had never seen, kiwi fruit and those strange "babacos". (I don't know how you eat such things!) We tried everything.

But times have to change! The children didn't want work in the greenhouses like us and off they went to look for work in town – and when we see the money they earn, cor chapin, they've done well. But all the same they have to get up and set out early, before it gets light, because of the parking. They eat their breakfast and shave in their cars, for if they arrive in town too late there are no places.

Here, the business is finished, as you see – with my rheumatism, I couldn't carry on repairing and painting – and the price of – oh, blow! my pipe's gone out!

Now let's see, what was I going to do? Ah, yes, there's my axe, I was going to chop you up. But when I think about it, I couldn't do you any harm. We have grown old together, you and I. You are the chronicle of my life! Oh, I'll clear up the rubbish another day. I'll leave you undisturbed in your corner. You well deserve your rest. Good-bye my old friend. If the worms come to eat you, may they do it gently!

Le Grànd Gallichan
par Harry Tomlinson

L'aout'jour j'fus au ch'nas pour trachier tchique chaose et quand j'y étais, j'trouvis aen viaer *Press*. J'c'menchis à llière et comme j'tournais les pages, j'vis la picture du "Grànd Gallichan" dauve sa faumme.

Caw chapin ch'en était-i yeun! Nous l'app'lait le "Grand Gallichan, mais i n'tait pas vraiment grànd, il'tait riocqué p'tit. Les gens li dounnaient chu naom-là parce qu'i s' creyait grànd. Tout chu qu'il avait et tout chu qu'i faisait était magnifique – suivànt li!

Vous le counissaites si est, ch'tait le p'ti Jerriais qui mariyit la fille d'Alfrat Pedvain juste oprès la djère. Vous savaïz, le sian qui bâtisit la grande maisaon auprès d'la choppe. Chapin, ch'tait aen vrai palais, dauve aen grànd "bathroom" atour aen "flush" étout. Oh, ch'tait tout "modern" vous savaïz.

Et ses greenhouses, il en avait des vérgies! Et les tamates qu'i creissait, caw, si nous le creyait, il 'taient grosses comme des caboches! Et son moto, nous érait dit que ch'tait lé sian d'la royne. Il'tait grànd et naer et il 'tait terjous bian polishi quand i sortisit le desmanche au saer dauve sa faumme. Et vous savaïz, ch'tait riocqué pour allaïr épiyaïr dans les spans de ses voisins pour veies comme tchique laeux tamates faisaient.

Et ch'tait li qu'acatit le prumier TV dans la paraesse. Caw, en était-i fiaer! Il l'avait dans l'endret dé d'vant et il djéttait tous les saers dauve les courtaennes ouvaertes pour que les passants véissent qu'il avait le TV.

J'vous dis, il'tait aen vrai vantaeux. Je n'sais pas d'ouéqu'i puchait, mais i bouillait d'sous. Bais il'tait comme tous, et quand ch'tait son tour, i muourit comme tous les aoutes. 👉

"Big Gallichan"
by Harry Tomlinson

The other day I went up into the loft to look for something, and whilst I was there I found an old *Guernsey Press*. I began to read it and as I turned the pages I saw the photograph of "Big Gallichan" with his wife.

Heavens, he was a right one! We called him "Big Gallichan", but he wasn't really big, he was only small. People gave him that name because he thought he was big. Everything he had and everything he did was marvellous – according to him.

You knew him yes, of course, he was the Jerseyman who married the daughter of Alfred Le Poidevin just after the war. You know, the one who built the big house by the shop. Lord, it was a real palace, with a big bathroom with a flush toilet as well. Oh, it was all "modern" you know!

And his greenhouses, they covered vergees, and the tomatoes which he grew, cor, if we believed him, they were as big as cabbages. And his car, one would have said it was the queen's. It was big and black and it was always beautifully polished when he went out on a Sunday evening with his wife. And you know, it was only to go and spy on his neighbours' greenhouses to see how their tomatoes were doing.

And it was he who bought the first television set in the parish. Cor, wasn't he proud of it! He had it in the front room and he watched it every evening with the curtains open so that all the passers-by could see that he had television.

I tell you he was a real show-off. I don't know where he got his money from but he was loaded. But he was like everyone else, and when his time came, he died like everyone else.

Quànd les gens virent chena sus l'Press, i dirent, "Eh bian, v'là le Grànd Gallichan parti," et y en avait étout qui dirent, "Tant mux!"

Mais ch'tait pas là la fin de l'affaire, parce qu'il avait arràngi l'enterrement d'vant d'mourir. Il avait chouaisi sa piaeche dans l'chaemtière draette d'vànt la muraile pour que les passants paissent veir la fosse et il avait mesme c'màndaï la pierre pour maette dessus. J'peux vous dire, ch'tait aen vrai monument!

Quand les haummes de Mess. Henry vinrent pour la maette sus la fosse, nous était tous raide ravi passequé l'affaire était si grànde – pus haoute qué toutes les aoutes dans l'chaemtière, et dauve enne sorte de pinaclle sus l'haout.

All'tait toute en rouge rocque, bian polishie, dauve son naom en or. Ma fé, all'tait vraiment magnifique!

Mais chu jour-là il écanchit qu'i c'menchit à plluvier, et la pllie caontinuit à tcheir toute la gniet et pour tchiques jours oprès, qui fait qu'la terre 'tait v'nue toute molle, et, veyous, chutte rocque-là était bian b'sànte, et oprès tchiques jours l'affaire c'menchit à càntaïr aen p'tit.

Ch'tait le Walter Tchéripé qui la r'mertchit, samedi au saer, quand i r'venait de cllaore ses spans. Quànd i la vit i pensit "Chena s'en va tcheir et a s'ra toute buchie. Ch'est aen piti parce que ch'est aen bouan morcé d'granit."(Vous savaïz, ch'tait pus pour l'amour d'la rocque que pour l'amour du sian dans la fosse!) Qui fait, i r'fut à ses spans et i trouvit du "wire" qu'il avait pour t'nir ses tamates à haout. Il pensit, "Chena f'ra l'affaire," et le v'là r'parti pour le chaemtière. Quand il arrivit, il amarrit aen but du "wire" à la rocque et l'aute but à enne grànd' arbre qu'était près de l' muraile. Quand il avait fini, i dit, "Chena tiendra pour aucht'haeure. Nous pourra telephonaïr à Mess. Henry lundi," et i s'en fut ciz li.

172

When people saw it in the newspaper they said, "Well, there's Big Gallichan gone," and there were also some who said, "So much the better."

But that wasn't the end of the matter because he had made arrangements for his funeral before he died. He had chosen his plot in the cemetery, right by the wall so that the passers-by could see the grave, and he had even ordered the gravestone to be put there. I can tell you it was a real monument!

When Mr. Henry's men came to erect it we were all really surprised because it was so big – taller than all the others in the cemetery, and with a sort of spire on the top!

It was all in red granite, beautifully polished, with his name in gold letters. My goodness, it was really magnificent!

But that day it happened that it started to rain, and the rain continued to pour down all night and for several days afterwards, so the earth had become very soft, and, you see, that gravestone was very heavy, and after several days the thing began to tilt a bit.

It was Walter Queripel who noticed it on Saturday evening when he was coming back from closing his greenhouses. When he saw it he thought, "That's going to fall, and it will be all broken. That's a pity because it's a nice bit of granite." (You know, it was more for the sake of the stone than for the sake of the one in the grave!) So, he went back to his greenhouses and found some wire which he had for supporting his tomatoes. He thought, "That will do the trick," and back he went to the cemetery. When he got there he tied one end of the wire to the gravestone and the other to a large tree which was by the wall. When he had finished he said, "That will hold for now, we can telephone Mr. Henry on Monday," and he went off home.

Le laondmôin ch'tait desmanche et les gens vinrent à l'égllise, et oprès l'service i sortisirent et s'mirent à d'visaïr d'vànt le grànd us, comme dé couteume. Les haommes étaient d'aen cotaï et les faummes de l'aoute, et il'taient à parlaïr de laeux tamates et des prix qu'il avaient iaeu, quand tout d'aen caoup le Wilfred Todvain c'menchit à rire. I riait comme aen perdu, et les aoutes dirent, "Tchiqu'il a daonc? Est che troubllai qu'il est?" Mais le paure Wilfred n'pouvait pas parlaïr parce qu'il riait tant, et chaque caoup qu'il éprouvit, il erc'menchit à rire.

"Mais t'es fou," dirent les aoutes, "pour tchi qu'tu ris comme chena, tchiqu' t'as?" Mais chaque caoup qu'i r'gardit le chaemtiere, le v'la erparti.

Finalement, quand il'tait aen p'tit pus tràntchille, il l'i d'mandirent, "Tchiqu' t'as que tu ris comme chena?"

Le paure Wilfred laeux mourtit la fosse du Grand Gallichan et dit, "R'gardaiz! Av-ous vaeu? Aucht'haeure il a le telephone!"

The following day was Sunday and the people came to church and after the service they came out and began to chat outside the main door as usual. The men were on one side and the women were on the other, and they were talking about their tomatoes and the prices they had had, when all of a sudden Wilfred Tostevin started to laugh. He laughed like mad and the others said, "What's the matter with him, has he gone off his head?" But poor Wilfred couldn't speak because he was laughing so much, and every time he tried he burst out laughing again.

"You're crazy," said the others, "why are you laughing like that, what's the matter?" But each time he looked at the cemetery off he went again.

But at last, when he was a little calmer, they asked him, "Why are you laughing like that?"

Poor Wilfred pointed to Big Gallichan's grave and said, "Look. Have you seen? He's got the telephone now!"

Aen p'tit accident
par *Hazel Tomlinson*

Georges avait passaï tchiques haeures dans aën cabaret dauve ses bottis et il'tait raide bragi quaend i décidit d'allair ciz li. Quaend il ouvrisit l'us pour sortir, i fut bian ravi dé veis qu'i plluvait avaerse et y avait des famaeux écllairs qu'i n'amendaient pas la situatiaon. I cryit "Bouan niet" à ses amis, mais i n'le ouirent pas car le tounnerre faisait tant d'cammas.

Il arrêtit enne minute su l'pas d'us pour décidair tchi qu'i s'en allait faire. I n'tait pas si bragi qu'i n'savait pas que sa faume s'en allait endjabiaïr le moment qu'i mourtait son nais autour l'us d'la cuisaine. Quaend il avait sorti d'la maisaon oprès desnair, il avait dit qu'i s'n allait ciz Jean Taudevin pour li d'mandaïr s'i pouvait empreuntaïr son faoux. Il avait en amas d'herbe dans l'couogn du gardin éiouqu'i voulait pllantaïr des caboches, et i fallait cllergir l'herbe d'vant préparaïr la terre. Sa faume avait dit qu'a voulait allaïr à la ville oprès desnair, et aucht'haeure i faisait niet – quaï haeure qu'il'tait? Il'tait en broue chu caoup!

Georges savait qu'il avait à tchittaïr l'abri du cabaret, mais s'il allait pour ciz li le laong d'la rue, i s'rait trempaï d'vant qu'i n'erait print enne douzôine de pas. Qui fait, i décidit d'allaïr à travaers du chimtière. Y avait en amas d'arbres là et ils le garderaient d'ête trop mouilli, et son ch'min s'rait raccourchi.

Tout fut bian au c'menchant. Les arbres le laong d'la rue le gardaient d'ête trempaï, mais quaend il entrit dans chimtière, le vent print son chapé et la pllie c'menchit à d'vallaïr avaout sa nuque.

A little accident
by Hazel Tomlinson

George had spent a few hours in the public house with his mates and he was quite drunk when he decided to go home. When he opened the door to go out, he was very surprised to see that it was pouring with rain and there were great flashes of lightning which did not improve the situation. He called "Goodnight" to his friends but they didn't hear him because the thunder was making so much noise.

He stopped on the doorstep for a moment or two to decide what he was going to do. He wasn't so drunk that he didn't know that his wife would scold him the moment that he showed his nose round the kitchen door. When he had left the house after dinner, he had said that he was going to John Tostevin's house to see if he could borrow his scythe. He had a lot of grass in the corner of the garden where he wanted to grow some cabbages and he had to clear the grass before preparing the ground. His wife had said that she wanted to go to Town after dinner; and now it was dark – what time was it? He was in trouble this time!

George knew that he had to leave the shelter of the public house, but if he went home along the road, he would be soaked through before he had taken a dozen steps. So he decided to go across the cemetery. There were a lot of trees there and they would keep him from getting too wet and his way would be shortened

Everything was fine in the beginning. The trees along the road kept him from being soaked, but when he entered the cemetery the wind took his hat and the rain began to run down the back of his neck.

Chena le marrit acore pus et i'n r'gardait pas éiouqu'il allait. Pour ag'vaïr l'affaire, i n'y avait pas d'leune et i pouvait justement veir les pierres des fosses mais… mal de grace! I n'avait pas vaeu enne fosse que le fossaeux avait préparaïr pour en' enterrement le laongd'moin! D'vant qu'i savait chu qu'i s'arrivait, il avait tchei dans la fosse! Mon dou sécours, il'tait vachi d'bâoe, et y avait pus que six pousses d'iaoue dans faond d'la fosse! Quaend i r'vint à li mesme, il éprouvit à grimpaïr hors d'la fosse, mais la terre était si moullie et la bâoe était si écrillànte que, oprés tchiques efforts, i baillit à haout et s'asseyvit sus l'faond dans iaoue. Il esperait que sa faume s'était couchie par chu temps, et qu'a n's'rait pas trop marrie quaend il arriv'rait ciz li finalement. Il éprouvrait à grimpaïr hors d'la fosse quaend i f'rait jeur. Le temps passit.

Apeuprès enn'haeure pus tard, i ouit en haume qu'i chantait et qu'i s'échoppait parmi les fosses. Saber dé bouais! Le perchoin moment, l'haume avait tchei dans la fosse! Ch'tait ieun de ses bottis! Mais il'tait si bragi, qu'i n'couunaissait pas Georges qu'était assis à aën but d'la fosse. Il 'eprouvit à grimpaïr hors d'la fosse mais, comme Georges avait trouvaïr hors, ch'tait impossiblle.

Georges li dit, "Tu n'sortira pas, tu sais."

Il l'fit, et bian vite, étout!

This angered him even more and he didn't look where he was going. To make matters worse, there was no moon and he could just see the gravestones but.... Good heavens! He hadn't seen the grave which the grave-digger had prepared for a burial the next day! Before he knew what had happened, he had fallen in the grave! When he had recovered his senses, he tried to climb out of the grave, but the ground was so wet and the mud so slippery that, after a few efforts he gave up and sat down at the bottom in the water. He hoped that his wife would be in bed by this time and that she would not be too angry when he finally arrived home. He would try and climb out of the grave when it was daylight. Time passed.

About an hour later he heard a man singing and stumbling about among the graves. Crikey! The next moment the man had fallen into the grave! It was one of his mates! But he was so drunk that he didn't recognise George who was sitting at one end of the grave. He tried to climb out of the grave but, as George had found out, it was impossible.

George said to him, "You won't get out you know."

He did, and very quickly too!

Enne lure Jerriaise
par Hazel Tomlinson

Y a à peu près en an qué enn' amie mé caontit chutte p'tite lure. Ieun de ses cousins était v'nu d'Jerri pour la veir, et enne seraïe i li caontit chutte p'tite histouaire.

La Daume Gallichan avait enne belle ferme dans la paraese de Saint Brelade. All'tait veuve dépis treis ans, mais ses daeux garcons aidjaient su la ferme dauve son bétail. A gogniait des coupes ès shaoux chaque onnaïe dauve ses vaques, mais ch'tait son magnifique boeu que tous admiraient le pus. Ses d'scendànts étaient envyaïs partout l'maonde, et quaend y avait enne caonférence atour la vaque Jerriaise dans l'île, tous les membres allaient pour enne visite à la ferme pour admiraïr le boeu et d'mandaïr des tchestiaons. Y en avait qui voulaient l'acattaïr, mais la Daume Gallichan savait chu qu'all'avait, et a voulait l'gardaïr passequé s'n haumme l'avait el'vaï treis ans d'vànt sa mort.

Le coumité pour le fermage li payait raide des sous chaque onnaïe comme écots pour faire servir son boeu sus la ferme d's Etats . I voulaient amendaïr la race Jerriaise et le boeu d'la Daume Gallichan était le millaeux dans l'île, n'y avait pas d'doute.

Aen jour, durant enn'assembllaïe du coumité pour le fermage, ieun des membres d'mandit s'il'tait possible d'acattaïr le boeu. Comme i dit, "J'sais bian qu'i coutra raide des sous à l'acattaïr, mais oprès chena, nous pourra chergier ès fermiers de l'île chaque caoup qu'ils le f'raont servi. Et pensaïz ès sous qu'nous pourra aver pour ses g'niches qu'nous pourra vende à l'Amerique et daoutes pays."

A Jersey tale
by Hazel Tomlinson

About a year ago, a friend told me this little story. One of her cousins had come from Jersey to see her, and one evening he told her this tale.

Mrs Gallichan had a lovely farm in the parish of St. Brelade. She had been a widow for three years, but her two sons helped on the farm with her cattle. She won many cups each year with her cows, but it was her magnificent bull which everyone admired the most. His descendants were sent all over the world, and when there was a conference about the Jersey cow in the island, all the members went on a visit to the farm to admire the bull and ask questions. There were those who wanted to buy him, but Mrs Gallichan recognised what she had, and she wanted to keep him because her husband had bred him three years before his death.

The Committee for Farming paid her a lot of money every year as fees for the services of her bull at the States' farm. They wanted to improve the Jersey breed and Mrs Gallichan's bull was the best in the island, there was no doubt.

One day, during a meeting of the Committee for Farming, one of the members asked if it was possible to buy the bull. As he said, "I know that it will cost a lot of money to buy him, but after that we will be able to charge the farmers of the island each time that they use him. And think of the money that we could receive for his heifers that we could sell to America and other countries."

Pus tard durant l'assembllaïe, i mit en d'vant enne propositiaon pour acattaïr le boeu. A fut passaïe, et l'haumme fut d'mandaï d'allaïr veir la Daume Gallichan pour li d'mandaïr si a vendrait son boeu ès Etats pour laeux ferme. Au c'mench'ment a r'fusit, mais à la fin, le coumité offrisit tant d'sous pour la bête que ses fils li dirent d'le vende.

Le grand jour arrivit, et le boeu fut print à la ferme d's Etats. Oprès tchiques jours i fut mit dans aen courti dauve des vaques, mais i n'tait pas interressi. I voulait riocque mangier l'herbe ou guettaïr les gens qu'arrettaient pour l'admiraïr. Les membres du coumité étaient en affaire – il'avaient dépensaï des milles livres sterlins du "budget" du Département pour l'Agritchulture pour tchi? Rian du tout! Oprès tchiques semoines, i criyirent au vetérinaire d's Etats, et li d'mandirent d'examinaïr la bête. I n'paeut pas trouvaïr autcheune choase qui pourrait expllitcher pourtchi qu'le boeu n'était pas interressi dans les vaques. Oprès tout, y avait dé ses d'scendànts partout maonde. P'tête qu'il'tait féniant.

Aen jour, ieun des membres du coumité rencaontrit aen viar fermier et li caontit la déjonie. Quaend i fut fini, i d'mandit au viar s'i pouvait sugéraïr tchique chaose qui leaux aigu'raït. Le vieil haumme l'vit sa câlotte, grattit sa tête et oprès tchiques moments dit, "I n'est pas fou, chu boeu-là! Ma fé! P'tête que nous n'peut pas l'bllamaï. J'creis qu'il a ouit que aucht'haeure i travaille pour l's Etats!"

Later on, during the meeting, he put forward a proposition to buy the bull. It was passed, and the man was asked to go and see Mrs Gallichan to ask her if she would sell her bull to the States for their farm. At first she refused, but in the end, the committee offered so much money for the animal that her sons told her to sell him.

The great day arrived, and the bull was taken to the States' farm. After a few days, he was put in a field with some cows, but he wasn't interested. He only wanted to eat grass or to watch the people who stopped to admire him. The members of the committee were worried – they had spent thousands of pounds from the budget of the Department for Agriculture for what? Nothing at all!

After a few weeks, they called the States' vet, and asked him to examine the animal. He couldn't find anything which could explain why the bull was not interested in the cows. After all, there were some of his descendants all over the world. Perhaps he was lazy.

One day, one of the committee members met an old farmer and he told him the rigmarole. When he had finished, he asked the old man if he could suggest something that could help them. The old man raised his cap, scratched his head and after a few moments, he said, "He isn't stupid, that bull! Good heavens! Perhaps we can't blame him. I think that he's heard that now he's working for the States!"

La breune
par Hazel Tomlinson

Y a à peu prés vingt ans qu'enne jonne faume arrivit dans aen p'tit village au sud dé l'Anglleterre. All'avait étai raide malade et son docteur li avait dit de prende aen holiday à tchique bord bian trantchille. All'avait trouvai enne p'tite caumaine tout près du p'tit port éiouqu'y avait enne vieille lighthouse. La tour avait étai abadounnaie pus que chent ans et persaunne n'y allait pas daute.

Au c'menchant a passit ses journaïes à marchier lé laong d'la banque et à exploraïr dautes villages et plliaches d'interêt, mais aen jour a pensit à la vieille tour. A d'mandit à ieun des vaisins s'a pouvait veis en d'dans d'la tour, mais l'haume li dit qu'all'tait toute ruinaïe et que les dégrais avaient tcheis. A chu temps a s'apperchut que y avait bian souvent enne tarrauere d'breune tard au sar, mais a s'était toute cllergie oprès miniet. A trouvait chena aen p'tit tchuriaux et a d'mandit à la propriétaire d'la caumaine si y avait enne raison pour chena.

"I n'faut pas se badraïr d'la breune. Yen a terjous lé laong d'la caute," et la faume n'voulit pas dire aute chaose. La jonne faume s'aperchut que la bruene c'menchait à v'nir d'la maïre chaque caoup à la mesme haeure – vingt minutes d'vant miniet. Pus étrange étou, à chu temps-là a n'pouvait pas ouïr lé corne à breune dé l'aute tour lé laong d'la caute et a c'menchit à aver paeux. A décidit qu'a voulait trouvaïr hors pourtchi qu'les gens du village n'sortaient pas au sar, ou, s'ils allaient à tchique bord, il'taient terjours ciz iaeux d'vant aonze haeures et d'mie.

The Fog
by Hazel Tomlinson

About twenty years ago, a young woman arrived in a little village in the south of England. She had been very ill and her doctor had told her to take a holiday somewhere very quiet. She had found a little cottage near a little harbour where there was an old lighthouse. The tower had been abandoned for more than a hundred years and no one went there anymore.

At the beginning, she passed her days in walking along the beach and in exploring other villages and places of interest, but one day she thought of the old tower. She asked one of the neighbours if she could see inside the tower, but the man told her that it was all in ruins and the steps had fallen. At this time, she noticed that very often there was thick fog late at night, but that it had all cleared after midnight. She found that a little curious and she asked the owner of the cottage if there was a reason for that.

"Don't worry about the fog. There is always some along the coast," and the woman wouldn't say anything else. The young woman noticed that the fog began to come from the sea each time at the same hour – twenty minutes before midnight. More strangely, as well, at that time she couldn't hear the foghorn from the other tower along the coast and she began to be scared. She decided that she wanted to find out why the people in the village didn't go out at night, or, if they went somewhere, they were always back home before half past eleven.

Enne journaïe a fut trachier dans les journaux dans la bibliothèque à la ville qu'était à vingt-chinq milles du village pour autcheune chaose qui pourrait expllitcher tout chena. Oprès enne laongue ercherche a trouvit enne histuoaire dans aen papier dé 1842 atour aen naufrage sus des rotchers pas bian llian du village. A chu temps-là, n'y avait pas d'lighthouse pour avertir lé captoine d'aen bâté que y avait des rotchers là. Et pière que chena, les gens des villages lé laong d'la caute allumaient des vaies quaend i taempêtait pour faire à craire ès captoines des batchaux en dangier qu'ils avaient trouvaï aen havre. Au reun i s'trouvirent sus les rotchers et furent niaïs. Pus tard, quaend i faisait millaeux temps, les gens du village allaient sauvaïr chu qu'i pouvaient d'la maïre ou dé d'sus la banque.

Mais tout chena n'expllitchait pas la breune ni la crointe des gens du village. Aen jour all'écanchtit dé rencaontraïr aen viar paissounnier qu'i li dit qué en 1842, des haumes du village avaient allumaï des vaies pour attraire aen bâté en dangier sus les rotchers. Toute l'étchipage muourrit mais lé captoine qu'était accore en vie maudit lé village et dit qu'i r'viandrait le hantaïr dauve s'n étchipage. Ieun des haumes du village dit que ch'tait enne rislaie et tuit lé captoine. Dé chu temps-là les gens qui d'meuraient là avaient aïe paure chaence et bian souvent y avait d'la breune au sar, à la mesme haeure que lé bâté tappit sus les rocques. D'écaute chena, bian souvent des gens avaient vaie des marriniers graïs à la vieille mode qui marchaient dans la breune enviars la lighthouse. I r'ssembllait qu'ils trachaient pour tchique chaose.

La jonne faume persuadit lé paissounnier d'ouvrir la tour, et i trouvirent aen viar cheste qui t'nait des hardes d'faume et d'bébi. Y avait étou enne picture qu'avait étai pointuraie d'enne jonne faume et aen p'tit éfant. I pouvaient faire hors lé naom au bas d'la picture: 'Mistress Anne Rogers and Child'. Lé viar paissounier fut étounnaï et dit, "Mais ch'est-là l'naom du captoine du bâté qui faonci en 1842! Enne jonne faume et son bébi furent trouvaïs niaïs dans iau chutte niet-là."

One day she went to search in the newspapers in the library of the town twenty-five miles away from the village for anything which could explain all that. After a long search, she found a story in a paper of 1842 about a shipwreck on the rocks not too far from the village. At that time, there was no lighthouse to warn the captain of a ship that there were rocks there. And worse than that, the people of the village along the coast lit lights when it was stormy to make believe to the captains of ships in danger that they had found a harbour. Instead they found themselves on the rocks and were drowned. Later, when the weather improved, the people from the village went to save what they could from the sea or from on the beach.

But all that did not explain the fog or the fear of the people in the village. One day, she happened to meet an old fisherman who told her that in 1842, some men from the village had lit some lights to attract a ship in danger on to the rocks. All the crew died but the captain, who was still alive, cursed the village and said that he would come back and haunt it with his crew. One of the men from the village said that was a joke and killed the captain. From that time, the people who lived there had bad luck and often there was fog at night, at the same time as the ship hit the rocks. Besides that, very often the people had seen sailors dressed in old-fashioned clothes who walked in the fog to the lighthouse. It seemed as if they were searching for something.

The young woman persuaded the fisherman to open the tower, and they found an old chest which contained the clothes of a woman and a baby. There was also a picture which had been painted of a young woman and a little child. They could make out the name at the bottom of the picture: 'Mistress Anne Rogers and Child'. The old fisherman was astonished and said, "But that's the name of the captain of the ship which sank in 1842! A young woman and her baby were found drowned in the water that night."

I décidirent dé matte lé cheste déhors la tour près d'l'us. Les r'venants pourraient le veis le perchoin caoup, et si ch'tit chena qu'ils trachaient, p'ete qu'ils prendraient et s'en irraient pour dé bouan. Chutte seraïe-là, la breune ervint. La jonne faume était derrière les courtines d'sa caumaine à djettaïr dauve le viar paissounner. Vingt minutes d'vant miniet, v'là la breune qui roule enviars le village. Aen moment i faisait plloine leune, et dans en'aute toute était env'lopai dans la mucreur. Et dans la breune les daeux qui djettaient virent les marriniers allaïr à la tour. Le sian qu'était à la tête vit l'cheste, l'ouvrisit et fit aen signe à daeux haumes. I l'virent le cheste en haut et s'en furent atour. Lé captoine s'tournit enviars la caumine éiouque les daeux djettaient. I leaux fit enne révérence et l'vit la moin – et disparut, breune et tout.

They decided to put the chest outside the tower near to the door. The ghosts would be able to see it the next time, and if that was what they were looking for, perhaps they would take it and go for ever. That night, the fog came back. The young woman was behind the curtains of her cottage watching with the old fisherman. Twenty minutes before midnight, there was the fog rolling towards the village. One moment it was full moon, and in another everything was wrapped in the moisture. And in the fog, the two who watched saw the sailors go to the tower. The one who was in front saw the chest, opened it and made a sign to two men. They lifted up the chest and went off with it. The captain turned towards the cottage where the two watched. He made them a bow and raised his hand – and vanished, fog and all.

L'endret
par Hazel Tomlinson

La Rachael Ozanne avait riocque vingt ans quaend a marryit Mess O'Reilly en dix-huit chents trente-treis. Souvent le marriage en Guernesi, a s'en fut dauve s'n haume pour l'Irlande eiouqu'i d'meurait. Sa maisaon était sus des côtis a peu près six milles d'aen p'tit village. All'tait graende dauve enamas d'endrets mais aen but d'la maisaon était tout frumaï et l'us de tuours était bouchi. S'n haume li dit qu'all'tait dangeraeuse et qu 'all'tait défendue d'y entraïr.

Y avait daeux servantes dans la maisaon, et quaend la Rachael l'iaeux d'mandit atour l'aute partie d'la maisaon i'n voulaient pas répandre et i r'ssembllait qu'il'taient effraies. Le temps passit, mais parfeis la Rachael se d'mandait tchiqu'était là, mais a n'y fut jomais.

Aen jour qaend s'n haume était parti au village et la Rachael était ennyaie et a n'savait pas tchi faire, a pensit à l'aute but d'la maisaon. A decidit qu'a voulait saver tchiqu'était là, qui fait a print aen chandiller et a s'en fut pour l'us qu'était bouchi. Y avait des pllanches cachtaïes à travers de l'ussrie et l'us était loctaï. La Rachael fut tcheure aen marté et a buchit les pllanches. A la fin a peaut entraï dans l'aute but d'la maisaon.

A s'trouvit dans aen laong passage dauve en amas d'us. All'ouvrisit tous les us mais dans tous les endrets ch'tait la meme chaose. Il'taient tous vièdes, et y avait en amas d'poussiere. A cantinuit frànc au but du passage eiouqu'a vit en'us qui n'avait ni puognie ni cllaie. A n'pouvait pas l'ouvrir! Par chu temps, raide guervaïe a fut a la cuisaine et a d'mandit ès servantes eiouqu'était la cllaie. I'n voulaient pas répandre qui fait a l'sit l'affaire.

☞

The Room
by *Hazel Tomlinson*

Rachel Ozanne was only twenty years old when she married Mr. O'Reilly in nineteen twenty-three. After the wedding in Guernsey, she went with her husband to Ireland where he lived. His house was about six miles from a village and was big with a lot of rooms. However, one end of the house was closed up and the outside door was blocked. Her husband told her that it was dangerous and that she was forbidden to go there.

There were two servants in the house, and when Rachel asked them about the other part of it, they didn't want to answer and it seemed that they were afraid. Time passed, and although she wondered about what was there sometimes, she never went there.

One day when her husband had gone to the village, Rachel was bored and didn't know what to do, she thought of the other end of the house. She decided that she wanted to know what was there, so she took a candlestick and went to the blocked door. There were planks of wood nailed across the doorway and the door was locked. Rachel fetched a hammer and smashed the planks. At last she was able to enter the other end of the house.

She found herself in a long passage with many doors. She opened each door, but it was the same thing in all the rooms. They were all empty but there was a lot of dust. She continued right to the end of the passage where she saw a door that didn't have either a handle or a key. She couldn't open it. By this time very annoyed she went back to her kitchen and asked the servants where was the key. They wouldn't reply and so she let the matter drop.

Tchiques semoines pus tard, la Rachael trachait tchique chaose dans aen viar cabinet quaend a trouvit enne vieille cllaie. All'tait toute rouie mais a chu moment-là a saie que ch'tait la cllaie pour ch't'us-la . All'aie à arretaïr d'autchet que s'n haume n'était pas à la maisaon. A print son chandiller et fut à l'us dans l'passage. All'éprouvit la cllaïe mais a'n'voulait pas tournaïr. A chu moment-là a ouit tchique chaose dans l'endret. Ch'tait aen p'tit effant qui plleurait. La Rachael tappit a l'us et cryit a l'effant mais a n'aïe pas d'rèpanse. Toute en affaire, a r'tournit à la cuisaine et d'mandit ès servantes quaï effant était dans l'endret. Les daeux faumes c'menchirent à plleuraïr mais i'n voulaient pas en parlaïr.

La Rachael mit de'l'huile sus la cllaïe et l'perchoin caoup qu'a fut l'eprouvaïr a réussit à ouvrir l'us. Biau qu'a t'nait son chandiller en haut, a n'veyait goutte. L'obscuritaïe était si épaisse qu'i r'sembllait que y avait des courtaines ou des irognies enter ielle et l'endret. A ouit tchique chaose qui bougeait, et parcqu'a voulait saver tchiqué ch'tait, al'entrit franc dans l'endret. La nércheur était pllione d'malice. Y avait d'la mauvaistché là -a pouvait quasi la touchier! Et pis a ouit aen mouvement – tchique chaose se troinait enviars d'ielle, a pouvait l'ouir respiraïr! À chu moment-là l'us darit et au meme temps... tchique chaose soufffllit la chandelle!

La Rachel disparut en 1923 et s'n haume tchitit la maisaon dauve ses servantes et n'y r'vint jomais. Qui fait, la maisaon fut entchierement abadounnaïe.Durant l'étai dé 1986, aen jonne haume et sa faume virent la vieille maisaon quand i s'pourmenaient su les côtis. I furent partout l'gardin et épiounirent par les f'netes, et i décidirent dé trouvai hors à tchique al'appartennait. I trachaient enne vieille maisaon à r'nouv'lair, et oprès tchiques semoines i ouirent qu'al'tait à vende. I pouvaient s'en affordair, et par la fin d'l'onnaie, il'avaient accataïe.

A few weeks later, Rachel was looking for something in an old cupboard when she found an old key. It was all rusty but at that moment she knew that the key was the key for that door. She had to wait until her husband was not at home. She took her candlestick and went to the door in the passage. She tried the key but it wouldn't turn. At that moment she heard something in the room. It was a little child crying. Rachel knocked on the door and called to the child but she had no reply. Very concerned, she went back to the kitchen and demanded of the servants the identity of the child in the room. The two women began to cry but wouldn't talk about it.

Rachel put some oil on the key, and the next time that she went to try it she succeeded in opening the door. Even though she held up the candlestick, she couldn't see a thing. The darkness was so thick that it seemed as if there were curtains or cobwebs between her and the room. She heard something which was moving, and because she wanted to know what it was, she went right into the room. The darkness was full of malice. There was evil there – she could almost touch it! And then she heard a movement – something was dragging itself towards her, she could hear it breathing! At that moment the door slammed shut and at the same time... something blew out the candle!

Rachel disappeared in 1923 and her husband left the house with his servants and never came back. So the house was completely abandoned. During the summer of 1986, a young man and his wife saw the old house when they were walking on the cliffs. They went all over the garden and peered through the windows, and they decided to try and find out to whom it belonged. They were looking for an old house to renovate, and after a few weeks they heard that it was for sale. They could afford it, and by the end of the year they had bought it.

Tout fut bian au prumier. I travaillirent dur, et oprès tchiques semoines il'avaient ramendaï la couverture et papraï des endrets. Aen but d'la maisaon était tout en ruine, qui fait i décidirent dé l'abattre entchièrement et faire aen gardin à sa pllache.

Aen jour,en ouvrier vint buyant à l'us.

"Missis! Missis! V'nai vite! Nous a trouvai tchiquechaose!"

I s'en furent vite veis et i furent gavlais quand i virent tchiqu'était là.Dans aen coin dé l'endret qu'il'taient à défaire, y avait enne stchélatte graie dans aen froc tout en chiques. En d'vant d'la stchélatte y avait aen chandiller dauve enne chandelle toute rogie. Et en d'vant dé chena y avait tchi? Aen mouchet dé plliau! Il'tait nar et couvart dé poussière. Mais tchiqué ch'tait? Enne bête – pas enne persanne absolument! P'tête qué ch'tait aen tchian ou aen guénan. Persanne n'savait. I n'avaient jomais vaie ditai tchet d'vant!

La stchélatte fut praïe ciz la police dans l'village, mais i fut décidaï d'enterrair la bête – ou chuque ch'tait – dans l'coin du gardin lé pus près dé chu but d'la maisaon. I s'ente d'mandaient tchiqu'i s'était arrivai là, mais i n'avaient jomais ouit d'la Rachel, qui fait.oprès tchiques meis i raombillirent tout atour lé tchian – ou l'guénan – enfin, la bête.

Tout fut bian pour aen p'tit. Mais laeux tchian c'menchit à bracqu'tair quand il'tait dans chu coin-là du gardin.Au sar i quinnait à l'us comme s 'i voulait allair touors. A chu temps étout ,la jonne faume c'menchit à sé sentir mal à l'aise dans l'gardin pour tchique raisaon quand all'tait dans l' coin éiouqu' la bête était enterraïe. I r'sembllait comme si tchiqu'un – ou tchiquechaose – la guettait. Mais quand a sé r'tournait pour veis, n'y avait autchun là.

Everything went well at first. They worked hard, and after a few weeks they had mended the roof and papered some rooms. One end of the house was all in ruins, so they decided to knock it down completely and make a garden in its place.

One day, a workman came yelling at the door.

"Missis! Missis! Come quickly! We've found something!"

They went quickly to see and were overcome when they saw what was there. In one corner of the room which they were demolishing, there was a skeleton dressed in a dress all in rags. And in front of the skeleton there was a candlestick with a candle which was all gnawed. And in front of that there was – what? A heap of fur! It was black and covered with dust. But what was it? An animal – not a human surely! Perhaps it was a dog or a monkey. Nobody knew. They had never seen anything like it before!

The skeleton was taken to the police in the village, but it was decided to bury the animal – or whatever it was – in the corner of the garden nearest to that end of the house. They asked each other what had happened there, but they had never heard of Rachel, therefore, after a few months they forgot all about the dog -or the monkey – anyway, the animal.

Everything went well for a little while. But their dog began to bark when he was in that corner of the garden. In the evening, he whined at the door as if he wanted to go out. At that time too, the young woman began to feel ill at ease in the garden for some reason when she went into the corner where the animal was buried. It seemed as if someone – or something – was watching her. But when she turned round to look, there was no-one there.

Enne serraie, i faisait biau fin d'leune. Lé jonne couplle était à soupair dans la cuisaïne. Tout d'aen caoup, lé tchian s'houlit caont l'us et c'menchit à quinnair comme s'il oyait tchiquechaose. Créyant qué y avait tchiqu'un à l'us, l'haume ouvrisit l'us et l'tchian s'en fut bracqu'tant dans l'gardin. I l'ouirent quinnaïr et pis i baillit aen cri qui g'lit lé sang dans laeux voines!

Lé jonne haume s'n allait suivre son tchian, mais sa faume cryit, "N'y va pas! Y a tchiquechoase là! Oh j'sis si éffraie!"

"N'té gène pas. J'm'en vais prendre m'arme."

"Quand même, méfie-té."

"J'lé f'rai. Reste-là, et locte l'us souvent dé mé."

Lé temps passit. Silence. Mais la jonne faume était effraïe. Eiouqu'était s'n haume? Pourtchi qu'i ne r'venait pas? Tchi qui était arrivai? A restit évillie à bas dans la cuisaine toute la gniet. A n'savait pas tchi en craire. Au p'tit jeur, tout douchement, all'ouvrisit l'us p'tit à p'tit et épiounnit dans l'gardin... Rian du tout!

A n'savait pas tchi faire. I n'avaient pas d'téléphaune accore. A n'pouvait pas criair à autchun. All'tait trop effraie d'coure à travaers du gardin pour s'écappair de – tchi?

A s'en fut à haut et trouvit aen morcé d'bouais qu'il'taient à faire servi dans enne chambre. A ll'mit caonte l'us' mais a n'tait pas saeure qu'i s'rait fort assai pour empêchier autcheune choase d'entrair. A s'assièvit dans enne gran'tchaire. Lé temps passit. A la gniet, a ouit tchiquechoase à l'us. Créyant qué ch'tait s'n haume – ou l'tchian, sans pus d'pensement ' all'étchippit lé bouais hors d'la vée... et ouvrisit l'us...

La vieille maisaon restit viède pour d'onnaies oprès qu'le jonne couplle disparut. Par chu temps, all'avait enne mauvaise réputatiaon. Y avait raide des gens qu'i pouvaient se r'maette d'la Rachel Ozanne qu'avait d'meuraï là dauve s'n haumme et qu'i entrit dans enn'endret qu'a n'erait pas daeu. Autcheun n'l'avait pas vaeue dépis.

☞

One evening, there was bright moonlight. The young couple was having supper in the kitchen. Suddenly the dog hurled itself against the door and began to whine as if it heard something. Thinking that there was someone at the door, the man opened the door and the dog went off barking into the garden. They heard it whine and then it gave a cry that froze the blood in their veins.

The young man was going to follow his dog, but his wife cried, "Don't go! There's something there! Oh, I'm so frightened!"

"Don't worry. I'm going to take my gun."

"Even so, be careful."

"I will be. Stay there, and lock the door after me."

Time passed. Silence. The young woman was very frightened. Where was her husband? Why hadn't he come back? What had happened? She stayed awake downstairs in the kitchen all night. She didn't know what to think. At daybreak, very slowly, she opened the door little by little and peeped into the garden... Nothing at all!

She didn't know what to do. They didn't have the telephone yet. She couldn't call anyone. She was too frightened to run across the garden to escape from – what?

She went upstairs and found a piece of wood which they were using in the bedroom. She put it against the door, but she wasn't sure if it would be strong enough to prevent anything from entering. She sat down in an armchair. Time passed. At nightfall, she heard something at the door. Thinking that it was her husband or the dog, without thinking, she threw the wood out of the way... and opened the door...

The old house stayed empty for years after the young couple disappeared. By this time, it had an evil reputation. There were a lot of people who could remember Rachel Ozanne who had lived there with her husband and who went into a room that she should not have done. No-one had seen her since.

Les onnaïes passirent. Le père du jonne haumme qu'avait disparut éprouvit à louaïr la maisaon ou mesme la vende, mais sans succés. Mais aen jour, i r'chut enne laettre d'enn' Améritchain qu'i voulait la louaïr pour enn'an. Il avait lu l'histouaire d'la maisaon dans aen magasin et, parce qu'il'tait enn'écrivoîn, i voulait v'nir en Irlande pour trouvaïr hors pour li-mesme chu qu'i s'était passaï.

La fomille arrivit dé l'Amerique à la fin du meis d'mai. Tout fut bian au c'menchant. Les daeux jonnes éffants oimaient à allaïr à l'école dans le village, et laeux mère passait son temps dans l'gardin. Laeux père était souvent parti à tchique bord pour trachier enn' histouaire ou à parlaïr dauve les gens du village.

Mais p'tit à p'tit la mère c'menchit à pensaïr que y avait tchique choase dans l'gardin. Tchique choase qu'i la guettait. Quaend a l'mentiounnit à s'n haume, i lie dit qu'il éprouvrait à trouvaïr hors tchiqu'y avait là.

I trouvit hors qu'éiouque sa faume pensait que tchique choase la guettait, ch'tait la tac éiouque l'endret était quaend la Rachel Ozanne avait disparut. Et pus que chena, ch'tait la mesme pllache éiouque les gens du village avaient enterrai la bête qu'il'avaient trouvaï quaend l'endret avait étaï abattu.

Durant l'meis d'juillet, la faume d'vint si effraïe qu'a n'voulait pas daoute allaïr dans l'gardin a son tout saeu. Les éffants n'voulaient pas y allaïr ni tout et i passaient enamas d'temps dans laeux chambes biau qu'i faisait magnifique temps déhors.

Les éffants c'menchirent à s'plloindre qu'i ouyaient tchiqu'un qu'i maontait les dégrais quaend il'taient dans laeux chambes, et il'taient effrais parce que, quaend i criaient à laeux mère, le camas arretait. Aen caoup, la pougnie d'l'us avait mesme c'menchi à tournaïr!

The years passed. The father of the young man who had disappeared tried to rent out the house, or even sell it, but without success. However, one day he received a letter from an American who wanted to rent it for a year. He had read the story of the house in a magazine and, as he was a writer, he wanted to come to Ireland to find out for himself what had happened.

The family arrived from America at the end of May. Everything went well at the beginning. The two young children liked to go to school in the village, and their mother passed her time in the garden. Their father was often gone somewhere looking for a story or talking to the people of the village.

But little by little the mother began to think that there was something in the garden. Something that watched her. When she mentioned it to her husband, he told her that he would try to find out what was there.

He found out that the place where his wife thought that something was watching her, was where the room had been when Rachel Ozanne disappeared. More than that, it was the same place where the people from the village had buried the beast which they had found when the room had been demolished.

During July, the woman became so frightened that she no longer wanted to go into the garden by herself. The children didn't want to go there either and they passed a lot of time in their bedrooms even though the weather was marvellous outside.

The children began to complain that they heard someone climbing the stairs when they were in their rooms, and they were afraid because, when they called to their mother, the noise stopped. Once, the door-handle had even begun to turn!

Le chinq de septembe d'vint enne date que la fomille n'raombillrait jomais. Chu jour-là, le temps était b'sant. I faisait aen caoud deviraï et 'le pid du temps était chergi d'orage'.* Parfeis y avait des écllairs. Les éffants étaient gergis et i n'savaient pas tchiqu'i voulaient faire. Laeux mere lavait les vaissiaux dans la cusaine quaend a vit tchique chaose dans l'gardin. Ou a pensit qu'all'avait vaie tchique chaose. Aen tchian? Nennin. Enne biche? Y en avait dans aen courti le laong d'la rue. Noufé. Ch'tait aen guenaon! Mais ch'tait pas possiblle! Il'tait 'naër comme du bloc'** et a n'vait jomais vaie ditaï d'tché d'vant. A criyit à s'n haumme, mais par le tmps qu'i vint à la f'nête, la bête était partie.

Chena décidit l'affaire. I tchittraient la maisaon le laon d'moin. Si restaient là pus laongtemps, ieun d'iaeux pourrait ête attatchiou pière. Nennin. I s'en iraient d'moin. Les parents c'menchirent à patcher tout laeux traffi et les éffants furent à haout pour tcheure laeux jouattes et laeux hardes. Quaend il'taient dans laeux chambes, i ouirent tchiqu'un qu'i maontait les dégrais. Créyant que ch'tait ieun d'laeux parents, la p'tite fut à l'us d'sa chambe. Chu qu'a vit l'éffriyit tant qu'a s'evonit.

A chu moment-là, en écllair égaluant et en graos caoup d'tounnerre tappirent draette en sus d'la maisaon. Le père print les dégrais treis au caoup pour tcheur ses éffants et i fut boulversaï quaend i trouvit la p'tite hors de counnissance. I la print à bas, dauve son frère, mais quaend il' arrivirent dans la cuisaine, sa faume li dit qu'a pouvait sentir tchique chaose qui brulait.

"Déhors, aucht'aeure, et pas d'ardjument," i dit a sa fomille, mais sa faume dit, "Le guenaon est dans l'gardin!"

I furent déhors et quaend i virent que le fait en glli avait print à faeu, i savaient que l'écllair avait tappaï la maisaon. Le père fut vite téléphonaïr à la brigade, mais n'y avait pas autcheune chaose qu'i pouvaient faire pour sauver la maisaon iaeux-mesme. A brulait bouan raide, et la fomille qui guettait, savait que tout s'en irait dans l'faeu.

☛

The fifth of September became a date which the family would never forget. That day, the weather was oppressive. It was terribly hot and it was likely that there would be a thunderstorm. Sometimes there was lightning. The children were fretful and didn't know what they wanted to do. Their mother was washing the dishes in the kitchen when she saw something in the garden. Or she thought that she had seen something. A dog? No. A goat? There were some in the field along the road. No. It was an ape! But that wasn't possible! It was black as pitch and she had never seen such a thing before. She called to her husband, but by the time he came to the window, the animal had gone.

That decided things. They would leave the house the next day. If they stayed there any longer, one of them could be attacked – or worse. No. They would go tomorrow. The parents began to pack all their belongings and the children went upstairs to fetch their toys and their clothes. When they were in their rooms, they heard someone coming up the stairs. Thinking that it was one of their parents, the little girl went to the door of her room. What she saw frightened her so much that she fainted.

At that moment, a dazzling flash of lightning and a loud thunder-clap struck directly over the house. The father took the stairs three at a time to fetch his children and was devastated when he found the little girl unconscious. He took her downstairs with her brother, but when they arrived in the kitchen, his wife told him that she could smell something burning.

"Outside, now, and no argument," he said to his family, but his wife said, "The ape is in the garden!"

They went outside and when they saw that the thatched roof had caught fire, they knew that the lightning had struck the house. The father went to telephone the Fire Brigade, but there was nothing that they could do to save the house themselves. It was burning fast, and the family who watched knew that everything would go in the fire.

☛

Tout d'aen caoup, le p'tit garcon criyit, "R'gardaïz, là, à la f'nête d' ma chambe!"

A enne f'nête au prumier étage, y avait enne persaonne à la f'nête!

Mais ch'tait pas enne persaonne – ch'tait enne bête, nère comme du bloc caonte les fllamblles dans la chambe. I r'sembllait qu'all'éprouvait à se sauvaïr. Et pis chu but-là d'la maisaon quaït et les fllamblles maontirent acore pus haout parmi des milles d'étinchêles. La bête avait disparut!

La brigade arrivit à la fin, mais trop tard pour sauvaïr autcheune chaose de d'dans la vieille maisaon. Au reun de l'orage, i plluvait avaerse, mais la fomille était sauvaïe.

Et la bête? Etait-alle morte? Etait-i possible qu'all'tait acore en vie? Tchi qu'i s'arrivit à la Rachel Ozanne en 1923, et au jonne couplle pus tard en 1983? Tout chena n'avait jomais étaï expllitchi. L'histouaire était-alle finie? Je'n'sais pas, mais si jomais j'trouve hors, j'vous dirai…comme de raisaon!

---

* A Guernsey idion
** Literally 'black as boot polish' – Guernsey idiom

Suddenly, the little boy shouted, "Look, there, at my bedroom window!"

At one of the windows on the first floor, there was a person at the window!

But it was not a person – it was a beast , black as pitch against the flames in the room. It seemed as if it was trying to escape. Then that end of the house fell and the flames rose even higher amongst thousands of sparks. The beast had disappeared!

The fire brigade arrived at last, but too late to save anything from inside the old house. Instead of the thunderstorm, it was pouring with rain, but the family was saved.

And the beast? Was it dead? Was it possible that it was still alive? What happened to Rachel Ozanne and the young couple? All that had never been explained. Was the story ended? I don't know, but if ever I find out, I'll tell you... of course!

Le policeman et les faies
Enn'histouaire de George Torode
racaontaïe par Hazel Tomlinson

Ch'est ichin enn'histouaire que le policeman Noël Trotter oimait a racaontaïr et que George Torode m'a bailli pemissiaon de traduire en Guernésiais.

Enne seraïe Trotter, comme il'tait counaeux, arrivit à la statiaon justement d'vant sept haeures. I s'n allait c'menchier son quart et il arrêtit enne minute à dire tchiques mots au sergeant en charge. A chu moment-là le téléphone sounnit, et le sergeant grounnit et dit, "Oh saber dé bouais, ch'est chu fichu Taffy derchier. J'll'ai dit chent caoups que je n' peux pas y aidgaïr."

" Tchiqu'i veur?" d'mandit Trotter.

"Arrête enne minute." répounit l'officier, et i print l'téléphone et dit:"Allo Taffy. Tchiqu'y a? I saont là derchier? J'ai l'gret mais je n'ai pas autcheun qui peut v'nir ciz té pour les attrapaïr. Si tu tourne ton wireless pus haout, tu n'les ouira pas daoute." I mit bas le telephone et dit à Trotter, "Tu counnis Taffy qui d'meure à St. Martin? Eh bian, tous les saers à sept haeures i m'téléphone pour me dire que les faies dans son ch'nas saont à faire du camas. J'en sis à but, j'peux te dire."

"J'irai l'veir si tu veur." dit Trotter, et i s'en fut pour St Martin sus son moto-bike. Quand il arrivit à la maisaon, i tappit à l'us, et oprès tchiques minutes enne vouaix dit, "Tchiqu'est là? All-ous en! Laissaïz-mé tranchille!"

"Ch'est la police, Taffy."

"J'vous ai dit d'vant. Je n'veur pas d'police dans ma maisaon! All-ous en!"

The policeman and the fairies
One of George Torode's stories
retold by Hazel Tomlinson

This is a story which the policeman Noël Trotter loved to tell and which George Torode has kindly permitted me to translate into Guernsey-French.

One evening Trotter, as he was known, arrived at the police station just before seven o'clock. He was going to begin his shift and he stopped for a minute to say a few words with the sergeant in charge. At that moment the telephone rang, and the sergeant groaned and said, "Oh blast it! It's that wretched Taffy again. I've told him a hundred times that I can't help him."

"What does he want?" asked Trotter.

"Wait a minute," said the officer, and he picked up the telephone and said, "Hallo Taffy. What's the matter? They're there again? I'm sorry, but I haven't got anyone here who can come to your house to catch them. If you turn up your wireless, you won't hear them anymore." He put the telephone down and said to Trotter, "You know Taffy who lives at St. Martins? Well, every evening at seven o'clock he telephones to tell me that the fairies in his attic are making a noise. I'm fed up with it, I can tell you."

"I'll go and see him if you like," said Trotter, and he went off on his motor-bike. When he arrived at the house, he knocked at the door and a voice said, "Who's there? Go away! Leave me alone!"

"It's the police, Taffy."

"I've told you before. I don't want the police in my house. Go away!"

Trotter pensit pour enne minute, et pis i dit, "J'sis aën policeman duràtnt l'jour, mais au saer et à la fin d'la s'moine, ch'est mé qui va attrapaïr les faies partout l'île. Vous n'savaïtes pas chena j'creis bian."

"Ah, chena ch'est different." dit Taffy. "Vous pouvaïz entraïr." Et il ouvrisit l'us.

I furent à haout des degrais, et Taffy li mourtit enne toute vieille étchelle qu'était arrànsaïe caonte la trappe du ch'nas. Trotter maontit l'étchelle souogniaessement car i croignait tcheir, et quànd qu'il avait fourraï sa tête et ses épaules par la trappe, i c'menchit à criyaïr, "J'peux vous veir! V'naïz ichin! V'naïz ichin!" et pis i d'mandit au viar haumme s'il avait enne grand'pouque. I s'en fut en trachier, et i r'vint dauve enne grand' pouque de papier de ciz Le Riche.

"Là," dit-i, "f'ra-t-alle?"

"Mais oui djà," répounit Trotter et i maontit franc dans l'ch'nas. I c'menchit à courre partout l'ch'nas en criyant, "J'peux vous veir là dans l'couogn. Là, y en v'là six, noufait sept. Cor chapin, y en a des douzoines! Dans la pouque!" I criyit à bas au viar, "Av-ous d'la corde pour amarraïr la pouque?"

Le viar trouvit aën morcé de boxcord et Trotter soufflit dans la pouque pour la faire enfllaïr et pis i l'amarrit dauve la corde. Quand il avait d'vallaï avau l'étchelle, i mourtit la pouque au viar.

" Les as-tu toutes?" d'mandit Taffy.

"I saont toutes dans la pouque. Vous n'eraïz pas daoute de brou." répounit Trotter.

"Merci bian," dit l'viar, et Trotter s'en fut sus son moto-bike dauve sa pouque plloine de faies.

Iaeux raide du pllaisi à la station chutte seraïe-là. Chaque caoup qu'en aute policeman arrivait là, Trotter fut oblligi de racaontaïr s'n histouaire de Taffy et les faies. A dix haeures, aen tout jonne policeman arrivit, et vit la pouque su l'contouaer.

"Lo, tchique ch'est chenchin?" d'mandit-i.

Les policeman dans l'endret criyirent tous ensemble, "N'TOUCHE PAS LA POUQUE!"

Vèy-ous la puissànce d'la parole!

Trotter thought for a moment, then he said, "I'm a policeman during the day but in the evening and at the weekend I'm the one who catches fairies all over the island. You didn't know that I'm sure."

"Well that's different," said Taffy. "You can come in." and he opened the door.

They went to the top of the stairs and Taffy showed him a very old ladder which was leaning against the trap-door to the attic. Trotter climbed the ladder very carefully for he was afraid of falling, and when he had thrust his head and shoulders through the trap he began to shout, "I can see you! Come here! Come here!" and then he asked the old man if he had a large bag. He went off to look for on and came back with a large paper bag from Le Riche.

"There," he said, "will that do?"

"Certainly," replied Trotter, and he climbed up into the attic. He began to run all over the place shouting, "I can see you there in the corner! There are six, no seven of them. Goodness, there are dozens of them! In the bag!" He called down to the old man, "Have you got any string to tie up the bag?"

The old man found a piece of boxcord and Trotter blew into the bag to inflate it and then he tied it with the cord. When he had come down the ladder, he showed the bag to the old man.

"Have you got all of them?" demanded Taffy.

"They're all in the bag. You won't have any more trouble." replied Trotter.

"Thanks very much." said the old man, and Trotter went off on his motor-bike with his bag full of fairies.

There was a lot of laughter in the station that evening. Every time another policeman arrived there, Trotter was obliged to retell his story about Taffy and the fairies. At ten o'clock a very young policeman arrived and saw the bag on the counter.

" What's this?" he asked.

The policemen in the room all shouted together,

"DON'T TOUCH THE BAG!"

Behold the power of the spoken word!

Quand j'étais jaunne: des souv'nirs du temps passaï
par Hazel Tomlinson

Oprès la djère, quand j'avais neuf ou dix ans, j'oimais à allaïr ciz ma tante et m'n aonclle à la ferme à Melrose ou ciz ma grand'tante ès Jehans. Duràent l'étaï, quand ch'tait le temps du fôin, j'oimais à allaïr dans les courtis dauve mes cousins et dautes éfàents oprès qu'le fôin fut fauchi.

J'creis bian que nous'tait enne fichue niésàence, parce qué nous oimait à s'muchier dans le fôin et à jouaïr des gaumes partout les courtis. Je n'sais pas comme tchi qu'les haommes évitaient de nous pitcher dauves laeux fourques à fôin quand il'taient à chergier le tchériot. Nous'tait allouaïs de maontaïr su l'haut du viage quand i fut print au ch'nas à fôin, et si nous'tait ès Jehans, nous pouvait, chatchun à son tour, maontaïr su la vieille jument Bessie.

Quand il'tait temps pour l'thée, y avait des caunnes de thée, d'la gâche à corinthe et des galettes doraïes de buon jaune burre qu'nous mangeait parmi l'fôin.

Pus tard dans l'onnaïe ch'tait la moissaon du bllaï et nous jouait parmi les djerbes. Parfeis nous y veyait des p'tites souoris mais quand les haommes venaient pour rammassaïr l'bllaï, y avait souvent des rats qui couoraient partout, et les tchians éprouvaient à les attrapaïr. Y avait d'la bractérie et de l'excitement – eh bian, et d'la crâqu'rie comme de raisaon!

When I was young: memories of times gone by
by Hazel Tomlinson

After the war, was I was nine or ten years old, I liked to go to the farm of my aunt and uncle at Melrose, or to that of my great-aunt at Les Jehans. During the summer, when it was hay-making time, I liked to go into the fields with my cousins and other children when the hay had been mown.

I'm sure that we were a blessed nuisance, because we liked to hide in the hay and play games all over the fields. I don't know how the men avoided pricking us with their hay-forks when they were loading the cart. We were allowed to go on top of the load when it was taken to the hay-loft at the farm, and if we were at "Les Jehans", each one in turn, had a ride on the old mare Bessie.

When it was tea-time, there were cans of tea, currant gâche and Guernsey biscuits spread with good yellow butter that we ate among the hay.

Later in the year it was the wheat harvest and we played among the sheaves. Sometimes we saw little mice but when the men came to gather the wheat, there were often rats that ran everywhere, and the dogs tried to catch them. There was barking and excitement – and well, chatter too, of course!

Chaque jour, à la fin d'l'arelevaïe, y avait terjous les vaques à traire. A chutte saisaon-là, ma tante les trayait dehors et j'oimais à la djettaïr et a lie d'visaïr durant la trair'rie. Parfeis j'étais invitaïe à aver mon soupaï dauve la fomille à Melrose, mais i fallait que j'fusse ciz mé d'vant la niet. Cor chapin, j'ped'lais mon byce comme enne troubllaïe amaont la rue de Plleinmaont parce que j'etais terjous tard!

La vie a bian changi, et j'ai l'r'gret que mes éfants n'pourraont pas maontaïr su les tas d'fôin et jouaïr toutes les gaummes qué nous jouait à chu temps-là.

I disent qué la vie a changi pour l'mux.

Je n'sais?

Each day, at the end of the afternoon, there were always the cows to be milked. At this season, my aunt milked them outside and I liked to watch her and chat to her during the milking. Sometimes I was invited to stay for supper with the family at Melrose, but I had to be home before dark. Gracious, I pedalled my bike like a mad thing up the road at Pleinmont because I was always late!

Life has changed, and I regret that my children will not be able to climb on to the hay-stacks and play all the games that we played in those times.

They say that life has changed for the better.

I wonder?

Chaslie et Jonny vaont à la ville
par Mabel Torode

La table est acore mise. Chaslie est assis à la table à llière le papier. La Florrie entre

Florrie   Avànche doan té, pour qué j'peuve cllergi la table. Quand j'étais sie men père, i nous disait qui fallait pas llière à la table. I disait qu'nous était là pour bère et pour mangier

Chaslie   Verre p'tete, mais ches pas sie ten père que t'es, ches sie me, et autchun n'me c'mandraont pas; et enne aute affaire, ches ma maisaon, et j'lé payie dauve mes sous et pas dauve les sous d'ten père.

Florrie   Naon, j'sai tout shena, mais i r'semblle à t'veis qu'tu n'as rian à faire. Eche que tu n'as pas vaeux la saerclle opres l'hus derrière? Tu n'as pas tànt serment l'tcheur dé r'parrai shena. Jenne sai pas tchi qu'les gens pense quand i viannent tappaï à l'hus.

Chaslie   Mais tu sai que l'docteur m'avait dit d'mé mefiaï, pasque, vé-tu, shute paompe la qui va à men tcheur, a travail pas acore trop bian.

Florrie   Eh bian, y a pas dangier qu'tie fashe de ma, pas à travaillier, pasque tu fais pas grand chaose. Mais avànche de t'quergi d'ilo, pasque j'm'en vais avait d'la visit sh'terlevaie, et j'veur en fini.

Charlie and Johnny go to town
by Mabel Torode

The table is still laid. Johnny is sitting at the table reading the paper.
Florrie enters

Florrie   Hurry up you, so that I can clear the table. When I
was at my father's house, he told us that we
shouldn't read at the table. He said that we were
there to drink and to eat.

Charlie   Maybe, but you are not at your father's house now,
you're at mine, and no-one will tell me what to do;
and another thing, it's my house and I've paid for it
with my money and not with money from your
father.

Florrie   No. I know all that, but to see you it seems that you
have nothing to do. Haven't you seen the weeds
near the back door? You haven't even the heart to
clean that. I don't know what people think when
they come knocking at the door.

Charlie   But you know that the doctor told me to be careful,
because, you see, this pump which goes to my
heart, it's not working too well.

Florrie   Well, there's no danger that you will do some harm
to it, not working, because you don't do much. But
hurry up and clear off from there, because I'm going
to have a visitor this afternoon and I want to finish.
☛

Chaslie   Orr, tchi qui s'en vian, eche la Royne?

Florrie   Nennin, ches la Lizzie. Sie yielle, y a pas rian par
           les cants, tout es à sa pllache. Ches pas coume
           ichin. Si tu halle enne cotte ou aen corset, ches
           houle sur enne tchaire; et tes bottes ou solers, ches
           sous enne aoute tchaire. Faut terjous que j's'rais à
           cllergi souvent de té.

Chaslie   Mais si tu n'avais pas shena à faire, tchi daon qu'tu
           f'rais? Tu s'rais bian onniaie.

Florrie   Mais vraiment noufé, pasque j'irais m'pourmenaï.

Chaslie   Eh bian, écoute. J'm'en vais à la ville, et i m'faut le
           livre de tcheques. Il est sans doute dans ta bourse
           pasque tu l'prend terjours dauve té; et bian shu
           caou ches men tour. Acore, opres tout ches mes
           sous qui saont à la banque, si y en a de l'si.

Florrie   Et bian v'la ma bourse là. Y a tchique billes dedans.
           J'cré bian en a assai pour té. Tu n'a pas couteume
           d'allai shoppaï. Si t'faut enne parre de caoushes,
           ches me qu'es oblligie de l's acattaï.

Chaslie   Je n'veur pas ta bourse, ches le livre de tcheques
           que j'veur.

Florrie   Et bian, tchi qu'tu t'en vas acattaï?

Chaslie   Te jaine pas de tchi que j'm'en vais acataï. Quand
           tu t'en vas pour la ville daeu ou treis caous la
           s'moine, je n'te d'mande pas tchi qu'tu t'en vas
           acattaï. J'm'en vais. A bietot.

Charlie	Orr, who is coming, is it the Queen?
Florrie	No. it's Lizzie. At her house, there's nothing lying around, everything is in its place. It's not like here. If you take off a coat or a guernsey*, it' s throw it on a chair; and your boots or shoes, it's under another chair. I always have to clear up after you.
Charlie	But if you didn't have that to do, what on earth would you do? You would be very bored.
Florrie	No fear, because I would go out to enjoy myself.
Charlie	Well, listen. I'm going to town and I need the cheque book. No doubt it's in your handbag because you always take it with you; well, this time it's my turn. Still, after all, it's my money which is in the bank, if there is any left.
Florrie	Well, there's my purse over there. There are a few pounds in it. I suppose that there's enough for you. You don't usually go shopping. If you need another pair of socks, I'm the one who has to go and buy them.
Charlie	I don't want your purse, it's the cheque book I want.
Florrie	Well, what are you going to buy?
Charlie	Don't worry about what I'm going to buy. When you go off to town two or three times a week, I don't ask you what you are going to buy. I'm off. See you later.

☞

Florrie Mais oyous. J'ensais tchi qui s'en va acattai. J'espère qui s'en va pas depensaï trop d'sous, pasque s'i mouorait, tous les sous qui saont à la banque, s'rait à me, et j'pourrais acattaï tout shu que j'voudrais, et j'pourrais avait de belles hardes coume la Dame du Gouvernaeux. (*Le telephone sonne*) "Hallo, ah ches te Lizzie- tu peux pas v'nit. Pourtchi?Ah, Jonny est parti à là ville et t'attends l'bouchier et bian, ecoute, j'm'en vians." Ches tché raide tchuriaux shena. Jonny est etou parti à la ville. Ches tché raide tchuriaux. J'm'en vais veis la Lizzie pour veis tchi que Jonny y a dit. J'trouvrai p'tete hors tchi qui saont à faire.

Courtaine
Chaslie r'viant

Chaslie Florrie, est tu par là? Jenne sai pas eiouque qu'al'est. A s'en vête ravie amesque a viannent. Al'est sans doute parti sie la Lizzie. J'espère que Jonny s'en va pas lie dire

Florrie r'viant

Florrie Ah, te v'là. Tchi qu't'as acattaï daon?

Chaslie Ah, mais ve-tu, j'm'en vais jouaï à golf, qui fait Jonny est v'nu dauve me et nous a acattaï ches clobs ichin pour y jouaï.

Florrie Mais tu n'sai pas tant serment coumtchi y jouaï. Et caombian qu't'as payi pour shena, 50 billes sans doute?

☞

Florrie   Well I never. I wonder what he is going to buy. I hope that he's not going to spend too much money, because if he died, all the money in the bank would be mine, and I could buy all that I would want, and I could have lovely clothes like the Governor's lady. *(The telephone rings)* "Hallo, ah it's you Lizzie-you can't come. Why? Ah, Johnny has gone to town and you're waiting for the butcher – well, listen, I'm coming." This is rather strange. Johnny has gone to town as well. It's very strange. I'm going to see Lizzie to see what Johnny has said. Perhaps I'll find out what they are doing.

Curtain
Charlie comes in

Charlie   Florrie, are you there? I don't know where she is. She's going to be surprised when she comes back. No doubt she's gone to Lizzie's. I hope that Johnny is not going to tell her.

Florrie enters

Florrie   Ah there you are. What have you bought then?

Charlie   Ah, well you see, I'm going to play golf, so Johnny came with me and we have bought these clubs to play with.

Florrie   But you don't even know how to play. And how much have you paid for that, fifty pounds no doubt?

Chaslie	T'entends 350 billes.
Florrie	Tchi qu'tu dit là, 350 billes? Eh bian, j'espère que Jonny n'a pas etai depensaï autànt, ou bian la Lizzie s'en va enjablliaï, j'en sie saeure.
Chaslie	Ah mais ve-tu, Jonny s'en va pas jouaï. I s'en viant dauve me pour portaï mes clobs, auterment j'érais iaeux à acattaï aen p'tit tcheriot qui m'érait coutaï enne aoute 100 billes. Mais, ve-tu, Jonny les portera pour erian, et i s'ra tout fiar d'ete hors de d'sous les pids d'la Lizzie.
Florrie	Arrete aen p'tit. J'm'en vais veis tchi qu'la Lizzie en dit de tout shenshin. J'sie saeure qu'a s'ra pas trop caontente de tout shena.
Chaslie	Eh bian, la v'là partie. J'm'en vais déhors pour pratitcher aen p'tit.

Charlie	You mean three hundred and fifty pounds.
Florrie	What are you saying, three hundred and fifty pounds? Well, I hope that Johnny has not spent as much, or Lizzie will be furious, I'm sure.
Charlie	Ah, well you see, Johnny is not going to play. He's coming with me to carry my clubs, otherwise I would have had to buy a little cart which would have cost me another hundred pounds. But, you see, Johnny will carry them for nothing, and he will be very pleased to be out from under Lizzie's feet.
Florrie	Wait a bit. I'm going to see what Lizzie says about all this. I'm sure that she won't be too pleased with all that.
Charlie	Well, she's gone. I'm going outside to practise for a bit.

---

* Traditional navy-blue fisherman's sweater

La servànte
par Mabel Torode

Quànd j'étais servànte sie la Daume Parmentier, enne belle seraïe auprès men jour finit, j'fûs pourmenaï le laong du douit, et y avait aen banc la, qui fait j'm'assievit la a mé r'posaï.

I faisait beau soleil qui j'pensit, "J'm'envais ête bian ishin pour la seraïe."

Au bût d'aen p'tit i s'trouvit aen biau gayiard q'etait bian graï, et raide faisànt. I l'avait aen haut box, aen biau bllu suit, des bllànc gànts et sen parapi.

I s'assievit opres d'mé et m'm'fie aen biau souris.

"Allo," q'im dit, "mon naöm chés James."

"Et bian," j'pensit, "j'fais mue d'lie dire q'lé mian chés Mary Jane."

Nous d'visit dé toutes sortes dé tché, mais j'pensit, "Faudra qué j'mé ramasse tandis qui fait jeur." Parcequé véious, j'étais pas accoutûmaie d'avait aen gayiard assis oprés d'mé. I l'appeurchi, et i m'enbrachi, j'vous en asseure qué j'étais éffraïe, mais au bût denne haeure, j'lie dit qu'il tait temps d'sé rammasaï. I'm dit, "Eiouque tu d'meure, ma vieille?"

"Ah," j'lie dit, "ches la bas sie la Daume Parmentier!"

"Et bian," i'm dit, "j'pourait marchiair dauve té, parcequé j'd'meure la haut sie la Daume Rouget!"

Et bian, nous sen fût, crotchit au bras, et quànd vint opres la hêche i m'enbrachit et i'm dounit aen biau gros kiss, épi i sen fût sûffiànt laöng d'la route, et savous qué j'en saöngit toute la benitte niet.

☛

The servant
by Mabel Torode

When I was a servant in the house of Mrs. Parmentier, one lovely evening after my day's work was finished, I went walking beside a douit (stream), and there was a bench there, so I sat down on it to have a rest.

It was lovely and sunny, so I thought,"I'm going to be fine here for the evening."

After a little while a handsome fellow arrived who was well dressed and charming. He was wearing a top hat, a blue suit, white gloves and had an umbrella.

He sat down near me and gave me a lovely smile.

"Hallo," he said to me, "my name is James."

"Well," I thought, "I had better tell him that mine is Mary Jane."

We talked about all sorts of things, but I thought, "I must go home while it's still daylight." because, you see, I wasn't used to having a fellow sitting near me. He came near and embraced me; I can assure you that I was frightened, but at the end of an hour, I told him that it was time to go home. He said to me, "Where do you live my dear?"

"Ah," I told him, "down there at Mrs. Parmentier's house."

"Well," he said to me, "I will be able to walk with you, because I live up there at Mrs. Rouget's house!"

Well, off we went arm in arm, and when we came near to the gate, he embraced me and gave me a lovely big kiss, then he went off whistling along the road; and do you know that I dreamed off it all the blessed night.

Lé lendemoin matin la Daume Parmentier paraisait pas trop fiere, et a m'die, "Os-tu, Mary Jane, éiouque tu fût passaï ta seraïe hiar au sàer? Il tait dix haeures quànd tu vint, et j'trouvis qué j'té raide tard, épi i mé r'sembllait q'javais oui la vouaïe d'aen gayiard." Au bût d'aen p'tit a m'die; "Os-tu, Mary Jane, tu parais malade, ou êche lassaïe q'tést?"

"Mais Madaume, jenne sie pas lassaïe, chest pûs a caou aen p'tit excitaïe! Véious, la vouaïe q'vous avaient oui, ch'té la vouaïe du James Lucas, car i vint m'condire dentche la hêche de bas."

Eh bian, au bût d'tchique jour le telephone sounit, et quànd j'oui la Daume Parmentier dire men naöm, j'pensit, "J'sie saeure qué ch'est James," et vraiment ch'té li. I mé d'màndit d'allaïr est pictures dauve li.

"Eh bian, faudra qué j'dmànde a la Daume Parmentier." Et j'lie d'màndit. A m'die, "Oui, mais faudra ête r'venu d'vànt qui s'rait niet!"

Nous s'enfût daön enne seraïe dauve nos bices, et quànd nous vint a la ville nous était bian lassaï. Nous s'assievit aen p'tit su aen banc au bût d'la cauchie, épi jdie a James, "Y'era pas d'pictures assésé car i faudra s'rammassaï d'vànt qui s'rait niet."

Nous sen vint tout laöng dés Banques, parcequé ch'té tout a pllàtt. Nous arreti a sé r'prende a L'ancraesse et au Vazon, mais quànd nous vint a L'Erée, ch'té toute en amaont dentche d'ête sie naön. Mais quànd nous fût gôgnit, James m'enbrachit et i'm baisi, et i'm'die, "Nous érait étaï mue assis toute la seraïe su nôt banc au bord du douit."

Next morning Mrs, Parmentier didn't look too pleased and she said to me, "Listen Mary Jane, where did you go and spend yesterday evening? It was ten o'clock when you came, and I found that it was very late; then it seemed to me that I had heard a man's voice." After a little while she said to me, "Listen Mary Jane, you look ill, or is it that you are tired?"

"But Madam, I'm not tired, more likely I'm a little excited! You see, the voice you heard, was the voice of James Lucas for he came to escort me to the bottom gate."

Well, after a few days the telephone rang, and when I heard Mrs Parmentier say my name, I thought, "I'm sure that's James," and so it was. He asked me to go to the pictures with him.

" Well I must ask Mrs. Parmentier," and I asked her. She told me, "Yes, but you must be back before it gets dark!"

So off we went one evening with our bikes, and when we got to Town we were very tired. We sat down for a little while on a bench at the end of the pier, and I said to James, "There won't be any pictures tonight we must go home before it's dark."

We came back along Les Banques because it was all flat. We stopped to get our breath at L'Ancresse and at Vazon, but when we got to l'Erée, it was all uphill until we got home. When we had arrived, James embraced me and kissed me and said to me, " We would have been better sitting all evening on our bench by the douit (stream)."